ANNABELLE SAMI   ILLUSTRATED BY DANIELA SUSA

Agent Zaiba
INVESTIGATES

THE HAUNTED HOUSE

LITTLE TiGER
LONDON

I

WELCOME TO OAKWOOD MANOR

"This is Agent Zaiba. Detective's log number five. The time is 17:00 hours. Location: Second-floor landing, Oakwood Manor. All entry points and emergency escapes have been located. Threat level remains low."

Zaiba clicked off the voice recorder on her phone and tucked it back into her pocket. Gazing out of the windows on the landing, she surveyed the grounds of Oakwood Manor and squinted into the fog. Whenever she came to a new location, she always made a general observation – getting the layout of the land and possible escape routes firmly in her mind. Being a secret agent meant being thorough and dedicated, even when it seemed nothing was amiss. She may have come here to hang out in her new friend's house, but an agent was never off the clock.

It was the first week of the autumn term and the days were starting to get shorter – darkness was already creeping in and they'd only got back from school an hour ago! The setting sun was casting long shadows against the high walls of the landing, and a slight chill in the air suddenly made Zaiba shiver.

"Zaiba! Have you finished your observations?" Poppy came running on to the landing, panting slightly. "Olivia said we can use her fossil-finding kit!"

Zaiba was relieved to see her best friend. "Yes, I'm all finished. Let's get excavating!"

"Exca-what?" Poppy looked puzzled.

"It means uncovering things."

Poppy laughed and poked Zaiba in the ribs. "You know all about uncovering things, Zai – especially mysteries!"

As the girls headed towards Olivia's room, Zaiba thought how lucky they were to have been chosen to look after the new girl during her first week at their school. They'd discovered that Olivia was kind (she'd brought them treats when her parents cooked something amazing), interesting (Zaiba had learned that the very last word in the dictionary was Zyzzeva – the name for a South African weevil!) and funny (her jokes made even their teacher laugh). In short, she was a fabulous new friend! *Maybe even a future member of the Snow Leopard Detective Agency UK branch*, Zaiba thought as they walked into Olivia's bedroom.

Olivia was setting up the fossil pit on the floor, kneeling down in the large tray, her soft red curls dangling round her face. The floor surrounding the tray was covered in sand.

A little bit of mess didn't matter too much though as Olivia still hadn't finished decorating her bedroom. There were squares of paint on the walls from where the Bookers had been trying out new paint and the carpet had been rolled up, exposing the bare floorboards. Olivia's new bedframe hadn't arrived, so she was sleeping on a mattress on the floor. Looking around, Zaiba noted the size of the room. It was so big and echoey that you could hear every tiny sound, from the smallest scurrying of a mouse in the attic to the scraping of a branch against the window...

The Booker family had only moved here at the start of summer and they hadn't got everything sorted yet, but they'd still managed to make it feel homely.

"I've set up the fossil-digging pit," Olivia beamed as Zaiba and Poppy came to join her. "It's just a big tray full of sand, but you can uncover some really good finds in it!"

Zaiba smiled at the way Olivia said 'tray'. She had a slightly different accent, which Zaiba loved. As her dad, Hassan, always said: "Difference is what makes life exciting!" Olivia had moved to their town from another part of the country during the holidays, so until school had started she hadn't had any friends to play with. It must have been lonely, but luckily Zaiba and Poppy were on hand now!

The girls set to work, picking up tiny trowels to begin sifting through the sand.

"How do your parents like it here, Olivia?" Zaiba asked. She decided not to ask anything about the scurrying sounds – after all, she wouldn't want them to think she was *scared*...

"They love the house and the woods around it! There's still lots of building work to do though and they're going to make some changes. They keep saying that the house is a diamond in the rough – whatever that means."

Zaiba knew all about diamonds after she'd solved her first ever mystery at the Royal Star Hotel. That, coupled with her success of uncovering a poison plot at her school's summer fete, had earned Zaiba her special agent stripes. It also definitely helped having Pakistan's top agent as an auntie. Aunt Fouzia had allowed Zaiba, her little brother Ali and her best friend Poppy to run the Snow Leopard Detective Agency's first overseas branch.

"Oh! I've found something!" Poppy squealed, clapping her hands.

"Here's the brush, be gentle." Olivia handed Poppy a wooden brush with long hairs and demonstrated how to push away the remaining dirt without harming the fossil.

"It's a... It's a..." Poppy squinted at the shape.

"Gastropod!" came a voice from behind the girls, making them jump.

Zaiba whirled round and saw her little brother pointing at the swirly shaped rock in the sand. "Ali, you shouldn't just sneak up on people!" she said.

"Neither should you, Flora!" Olivia wagged her finger at her younger sister, who was hiding behind Ali. Flora also had ginger hair, though she had it cut into a wavy bob. Both girls had bright green eyes and round faces – Flora was basically a mini version of her sister.

"Looks like a marine gastropod to me," Flora added, taking a closer look at the fossil. Even though she was only eight years old, Flora had an impressive range of knowledge – just like Ali! It wasn't surprising that Ali and Flora had become firm friends. "But what's that?"

Flora pointed at another lump in the sand, and just as her finger grazed the surface ... it moved!

"A mouse!" The group screamed, running to the corners of the room.

There was a sudden pounding of footsteps and then Olivia and Flora's mum, Courtney, appeared at the door, red-faced and breathless.

"What's going on?" she panted. "I heard screaming!"

"There was a mouse, Mum!" Flora was horrified, and Zaiba had to admit her own heart was beating very fast.

"I think it's scampered away into a little hole behind the cupboard." Olivia had wriggled behind the wooden cupboard checking it out, which earned her a lot of bravery points in Zaiba's opinion.

Courtney sighed and steadied herself against the doorframe. "Oh, just a mouse. We'll have to put down some humane traps... I'm just glad it wasn't the—" Courtney stopped herself. "Never mind. Tea will be ready soon, we're having a pizza feast!"

Forcing a smile, she left the room and headed back down the squeaky stairs.

"Yes, pizza!" Poppy had quickly recovered from the shock of the mouse with the mention of one of her absolute favourite things – food! "Yum! I wonder if it's a sourdough crust..."

Even though her foodie friend seemed happy enough, Zaiba knew something wasn't right. A good detective could sense when there was mystery in the air.

"Is your mum OK, Olivia? She seemed really worried." Zaiba knew to be delicate. When asking a potential source for information, you had to be careful not to push too hard.

Olivia's expression darkened and she beckoned for them to come closer. Ali and Flora moved nearer too, huddling into a circle on the bare wood floor.

"Well," Olivia whispered, "Mum told me not to mention it, but since you're detectives, I don't think you'll be scared. After everything you've told me at school about the cases you've solved, I know you'll be able to handle it."

Zaiba's heart began to beat a little faster. "Scared of what?"

Olivia and Flora exchanged a look.

"Mum thinks the house is haunted," Flora said, rolling her eyes.

"I do too!" Olivia blurted out. Flora shot her older sister

9

a stern glance, but Olivia carried on. "I mean, we've found plates smashed in the kitchen and a vase knocked on to the floor in the foyer, furniture has been moved around ... even some of Mum's jewellery has gone missing!"

Poppy gasped in horror and Zaiba's mind was racing a mile a minute. She *knew* she'd felt a strange atmosphere here! Despite the obvious worry, Zaiba couldn't help but feel slightly relieved that her detective instincts were still strong.

"Is there anything we can do to help?" Zaiba asked. She liked Olivia's family and it seemed that all this drama was making Courtney super stressed.

"Not unless you know how to stop the ghosts being so troublesome," Olivia said gravely. "I heard an old lady in the village shop talking about how this house was used for injured World War One soldiers to recover in."

Flora stood up and brushed the sand from her denim skirt. "For goodness' sake, Liv. It's not a ghost!" She looked at Ali and shrugged. "They're just accidents."

Ali nodded in agreement. "From a scientific point of view, there is absolutely no hard evidence to prove that ghosts exist."

"As a detective, Zaiba, you must trust the science?" Flora appealed to Zaiba.

Zaiba took in the collection of faces looking at her. "I can't come to a conclusion until I've made a thorough investigation." She crossed her arms to show Ali and Flora she meant business and Poppy crossed hers too in support.

Now it was Ali's turn to roll his eyes. "But Zaiba—"

"But nothing! I've heard too many ghost stories from our Pakistani family at parties about evil jinn... Why would so many people make something like that up? Aunt Fouzia even said she *saw* a jinn when she was a little girl. It stole a banana from her kitchen table! Aunt Fouzia wouldn't lie to me."

"Is a jinn like a ghost?" Olivia asked, anxiously looking round the room for any lurking shadows.

"Basically." Zaiba nodded. "They can be good or bad, helpful or mischievous. But even if these events aren't caused by a ghost, we simply *have* to investigate. Flora could be right. Maybe they are accidents." She paused.

"And maybe they aren't. What do you think, Pops?"

Poppy was chewing her nails, so Zaiba could tell she was frightened. Poppy didn't ruin her manicure for just anything! She thought for a little while and then took a deep breath, drawing herself up tall. "I think it's our duty to figure this out! Does this mean the Snow Leopard Detective Agency UK have their next case?"

Olivia's eyes widened in anticipation and Zaiba knew what she had to do.

"Olivia, we would like to investigate the case of your haunted house."

Olivia threw her arms round Poppy and Zaiba in a big hug. "Oh, thank you, thank you! I like it here. I don't want my mum to get so scared that we have to move. Even Dad's been getting a little bit freaked out..."

Ali cleared his throat. "In the interests of scientific balance, I'd like to help with the investigation too."

"Me too!" Flora said, then quickly added, "If you'll let me."

"Of course!" Poppy smiled. "And Olivia too."

"The more brains the better." Zaiba agreed. "I'm sure

there's a logical explanation to all this." Though she still felt uneasy in her tummy, as if she was trying to convince herself more than the others. "But when can we begin the investigation? My dad is coming to pick us up after dinner."

Olivia thought for a while, her green eyes focusing in concentration. She clicked her fingers. "I know! My parents are having a housewarming party tomorrow. Why don't you and your parents come too? You can sleep over and we can start looking for clues."

"Perfect!" Zaiba nodded. "If you're sure your mum won't mind. Ali, you and I will get our equipment ready at home. Poppy, do you still have that copy of Eden Lockett's *The Haunting of Hay Hall* I lent you? There are some useful notes from my ammi in it that we might need."

Eden Lockett was Zaiba and Poppy's favourite author – a real-life detective who wrote about the mysteries she solved in a series of books. Zaiba had inherited a huge collection of Eden Lockett books from her birth mum who had gone missing years ago. Bit by bit, Zaiba was piecing together the mystery of who her ammi was by reading notes she had left in the margins of the books. Zaiba had only just learned that her ammi and Aunt Fouzia had set up the Snow Leopard Detective Agency in Karachi together! Detecting ran in Zaiba's blood.

"Don't worry, Olivia and Flora. We're on the case. Together we can solve this!" Zaiba put her hand in the middle of the circle and, one by one, her friends placed their hands on top. "What shall we say on three?"

Ali's eyes lit up and there was a cheeky smile on his face. "I know!

"One...

"Two...

"Three...

"Boo!"

2
PREPPING FOR THE POLTERGEIST

It was Saturday morning and Zaiba woke up with a sense of purpose (and just the *slightest* tummy ache from all the pizza they'd eaten last night).

She glanced over at the shiny white desk in the corner of her bedroom with the matching white leather swivel chair. She'd asked for the desk as a birthday present since she knew how important it was for a detective to have a place to organize her case files. With the colour-coded files and stationery trays, the desk had become the perfect headquarters for the Snow Leopard Detective Agency UK! Together with Poppy and Ali, they had come up with their own logo and used cardboard and craft paper to make a sign, which they hung over the desk. It was a snow leopard's face in profile, mouth open in a roar, against a black background. Underneath they had stuck on the letters S.L.D.A. UK (since the angecy name was too long to write out in full).

To keep a record of the cases they'd cracked so far, Zaiba had pinned up a large corkboard behind her desk. Stuck in with a gold pin was a piece of bunting from the cake-baking tent at her school's summer fete, where Zaiba and the team had discovered who had baked a poisoned cupcake! Next to it was the map from the Royal Star Hotel, where they'd solved the case of the missing diamond dog collar.

Now Zaiba smiled. When she'd shown the desk and sign to Aunt Fouzia during a video call, her aunt had said it looked just as professional as the desk she had in her office in Karachi.

Pushing back her Eden Lockett bed sheets, decorated in tiny footprints and a large magnifying glass, Zaiba stretched and brushed her wavy hair from her eyes. Straightening out her pastel blue nightgown, she swung her legs out of bed and walked over to her desk. She wanted to admire the folder she had made *one more time* before breakfast. Even though it had been late when Zaiba finally got up to her room last night, she wanted to be ready for the investigation today. She'd found a brand-new laminated black folder and stuck a label down the side, writing in clear capitals: THE HAUNTED HOUSE, OAKWOOD MANOR. It had a section for evidence, notes and transcripts of the voice recordings she would take on her phone. It was *perfect*.

"Zaiba! Are you up? Poppy will be here soon!" called Zaiba's stepmum, Jessica. A faint hiss of frying butter let Zaiba know that Jessica was making her favourite breakfast – blueberry pancakes! Just what a young detective needed to prepare for a long day of investigating.

Zaiba quickly popped into the bathroom, kicking Ali out for taking too long.

"I want to look smart for the party!" he complained.

"I need five more minutes!"

"You'll need longer than that to make this look smart," Zaiba teased, ruffling Ali's long curly fringe.

After a quick shower, Zaiba was standing in front of her wardrobe trying to decide what to wear for the party later. It was impossible to choose from the tangle of clothes in her cupboard. Luckily her own personal stylist came running up the stairs. On Saturday mornings, Poppy's mum Emma played netball with her friends, so Poppy had come over early to help prepare for the investigation with Ali and Zaiba.

"That dark orange shalwar kameez!" Poppy pointed at the tunic hanging in Zaiba's wardrobe. "That colour is really in this season."

Zaiba pulled it out and held it up to her, looking in the mirror. "We are going to a party, and I trust you on anything to do with fashion!"

Poppy straightened her own forest-green skirt and T-shirt in the mirror. Zaiba pulled on some jeans and a jumper and packed the shalwar kameez away for later.

Poppy showed her how to roll it up so it wouldn't

crease. "My mum taught me this trick. It's how I've packed my party dress into my bag for later," she explained.

"Are you decent?" Ali said, knocking at the door and shielding his hands with his eyes.

"Yes, come in," Zaiba laughed. "And don't forget I used to help Mum bathe you when you were a baby."

Ali stuck his tongue out. "Don't remind me! Now where are we with preparations for investigation 'Prove Ghosts Aren't Real'?"

"Ali, keep an open mind. *A good detective weighs up all the options.* That's Eden Lockett's golden rule number three."

Zaiba patted the overnight bag she'd packed specially for the occasion. Aside from her party dress and all her regular sleepover essentials, it also contained her Eden Lockett binoculars,  a notepad and pen, tape measure, a torch, a first-aid kit and some rope. After she'd had to scale a wall in her first investigation, she thought it was better to be safe than sorry!

"We're all set. There's just one thing left to do."

Down in the kitchen, where a big plate of pancakes with blueberries and syrup was waiting, Jessica had set up her laptop for Zaiba, Ali and Poppy to video call one of Zaiba's favourite people in the whole world – her cousin, Samirah.

Sam was a junior doctor, recently married to Tanvir (#SamTan forever), and Aunt Fouzia's daughter. She was like a big sister to Zaiba. Sam had texted Zaiba's dad Hassan that morning to say she had exciting news to share, and Zaiba was desperate to find out what it was.

"So, my budding detectives! How are you today?" Sam asked, her beautiful smile filling the computer screen.

Ali, Zaiba and Poppy started to babble at the same time.

"There's a ghost at Oakwood Manor!"

"We're starting a new investigation—"

"—prove once and for all that there's a logical explanation!"

Sam took a big breath in, her eyes darting around the screen as she tried to keep track of who was talking. She held up her hands. "Wow! Hold on, hold on. This is a lot to take in." She grinned. "And I haven't even told you my news yet!"

Suddenly a new face appeared on the screen, blocking out Sam with a dazzling smile.

"Aunt Fouzia!" Zaiba, Ali and Poppy chorused. It was their favourite detective auntie!

Aunt Fouzia waved at them. "That's right, sweeties! I flew all the way from Karachi to surprise you." She winked before Sam pushed her back out of the way.

"Ammi, that isn't the surprise, remember?" Sam looked exasperated although she couldn't help chuckling. "Can you guys figure out what it is? You're all such brilliant detectives."

Poppy had a go first. "Is it that Aunt Fouzia has brought us some delicious sweets back from Pakistan?"

Zaiba rolled her eyes. Poppy's first thoughts were almost always food-related.

Sam shook her head. "Nope! Try again."

Poppy slumped on her stool but Ali's hand shot into the air. "Is it that you're on the brink of a ground-breaking new scientific discovery in the world of medicine?" His eyes shone, thinking of the possibilities.

"Not quite. Sorry, Ali." Sam winked. "Zaiba?"

Zaiba bit her lip and thought hard. She was sure she knew what the news was, but she didn't know if it was rude to say.

"Well, Sam... I have noticed that you've not been running like you used to. You don't eat eggs any more and when we went for your birthday dinner you made sure all the meat was cooked really well. Plus you've been wearing baggier clothes than usual. So, are you having a baby?"

Sam clapped her hands together. "You really are a brilliant detective, Zaiba. I should have known you'd guess. Yes, I'm pregnant!"

"And I'm going to be a grandma!" Aunt Fouzia called happily from off-screen.

All three of them cheered and Poppy burst out in a round of applause. Jessica and Hassan, who were sitting at the other end of the table, smiled knowingly at each other.

Why is it that grown-ups just seem to know things sometimes? Zaiba thought. But that didn't stop her from being thrilled at Sam's news ... and that she'd got to show off her detective skills in front of Aunt Fouzia.

"So, your aunt Fouzia is staying with me until the baby arrives!" Sam explained.

"Oh my gosh, this is so exciting!" Poppy sang. "Think of all the cute baby outfits we can get for her."

"We don't know if it's a girl yet, Poppy," Aunt Fouzia said from off-camera.

"How about Eden for a name?" Zaiba suggested.

"Or Ali!" Her little brother raised a finger. "I will be the baby's favourite relative, of course."

Sam waved her hands in a slow-down motion. "The baby isn't due for another four months. I'm excited too, but I have to stay calm. I can't even drink caffeine any more and you know how much I love my *chai*. Hot water and lemon just isn't the same..."

Zaiba felt a little sorry for her cousin. It sounded like there were lots of rules involved with being pregnant. But at least this meant Zaiba was going to have a brand-new baby to play with!

"Besides, don't you have other matters to focus on first?" Sam wiggled her eyebrows.

Aunt Fouzia leaped in front of the camera. "Yes, the mystery at Oakwood Manor. Keep your eyes and ears peeled, team! At night things can be harder to detect. Make sure your torches are fully charged and catch that ghost. OooooOoo." Aunt Fouzia made ghostly howling noises as they waved goodbye and hung up.

Ali put his face in his hands. "Not Aunt Fouzia too!"

Hassan put down his newspaper and rescued the laptop, storing it safely back in a drawer. "Your aunt Fouzia tells the scariest stories about jinn, ghosts and ghouls. She used to scare Zaiba's ammi silly!"

Zaiba considered this. Knowing her ammi was scared of jinn made her feel better about getting spooked at Oakwood Manor. Whenever Zaiba learned more information about her birth mum, she quickly filed it away in her brain to remember for later. Hassan would tell Zaiba the occasional detail like how she had inherited her ammi's loud laugh, or that she made the best cup of chai he'd ever tasted, but he didn't focus much on ammi's detective work. After all, she had gone missing while on a mission. Zaiba loved Jessica, but she did miss her ammi and sometimes she dreamed about having a mum who shared her passion for detecting.

However there was no time for pondering now. They had a case to solve! Olivia would be waiting for them to arrive to begin the investigations.

"I think we should get going," Ali said, hastily glancing at his watch. "It takes precisely fourteen minutes to drive to Oakwood Manor, providing we stay at the speed limit and traffic is moderate."

Jessica laughed and patted Ali on the head. "Hassan will drop you off. I've got some shopping to do. I want to bring a nice housewarming present."

Poppy stuck out her bottom lip. "I wish I could come. I love shopping."

Zaiba laughed and grabbed her friend's hand, pulling her out of the door. "Shopping can wait. We've got a ghost to catch!"

Ali (as usual) was correct in his predictions. The drive to Olivia's house took thirteen minutes and fifty-eight seconds. They didn't pass many neighbours since Oakwood Manor was so out of the way. But Zaiba could have sworn she saw a pair of eyes peering round the curtain of the last house on the road before they turned on to the long driveway that led to the manor. As they pulled up, Hassan whistled. It was the first time he'd seen the place.

"I know why they call it a manor now," he said as he took in the huge brick facade, with its numerous windows and pointed slate roof. Zaiba pressed her face to the car window and sensed the eerie feeling creep back over her. Oakwood Manor must have been impressive when it was first built, but the sharp angles of the roof and the ivy that had grown over the crumbling bricks now made it appear deserted, despite its new residents. Hassan poked his head out of the window to say hello to Olivia's parents, who had come to the door.

"Do you need a hand with anything?" he called. But Courtney had already come out to help the kids. With her round cheeks, small chin and green eyes she looked almost like a fairy.

"No, no it's fine. Don't worry!" She smiled, passing the bundled-up sleeping bags to her husband Jack, who had joined her in the driveway. Courtney had blond hair, but Jack's was fiery red and curly.

"Have fun! Behave yourselves!" Hassan wagged a finger at Zaiba and the others.

"Isn't that a contradiction in terms?" Ali muttered.

Zaiba elbowed him. "Just wave goodbye," she said out the side of her mouth. The sooner their dad was off, the sooner they could start their investigation. They all waved as Hassan drove back down the gravel driveway, tyres crunching on the uneven stones.

Olivia ran out to greet them. "Hello! Do you want to see the sleepover set-up in my room?"

"Yes please!" Zaiba and Poppy cried.

"Does it have a computer?" Ali asked.

All four of them ran into the house where the party prep was under way. A hoover was parked in the middle of the huge foyer and a bottle of polish with a rag had been left on the oak-wood staircase. Even with the lights on, the foyer was dim and the hard, shiny flooring made

Zaiba feel cold. She was glad to follow Olivia up to her room, where her mum had set up five roll-out foam mattresses. Luckily Olivia's room was massive. It even had an old fireplace and a glass chandelier!

Zaiba and Poppy laid out their matching Eden Lockett sleeping bags. Zaiba's was a pastel blue to match her nightgown and Poppy's was pink – her absolute favourite colour. The sleeping bags had special secret compartments at the bottom to hide your valuables in and the zip was shaped like a magnifying glass!

"Why do I have to use Dad's old camping stuff?" Ali grumbled, fumbling with a huge sleeping bag. "It's five times bigger than me!"

"I know how you feel. I have Olivia's old pony duvet." Flora stuck her tongue out in disgust at the glittery design.

Zaiba, Poppy and Olivia giggled.

"This is going to be so much fun!" Olivia beamed as she admired their sleepover set-up.

But Zaiba's mind was back on the task at hand. "I'd like to start by taking a sweep of the grounds around the house, please, Olivia," she announced. "With woods like these, you can't be too careful. Anyone could approach ... unseen."

Poppy nodded seriously and gathered the others round her. "Is everyone ready?" She glanced from face to face, checking. "Are you *sure* you're ready?"

The others nodded and looked at each other, slightly confused.

Poppy threw out her arms dramatically. "We're about to go ghost hunting!"

3
IN A DARK, DARK WOOD

Zaiba led Olivia and Poppy downstairs, patting her little backpack. She needed to make sure she'd brought everything she needed! Ali and Flora had already rushed ahead.

"Detective's log number one of the investigation of Oakwood Manor. The time is 11:30 hours and we are beginning our search in the woods." Zaiba glanced round at her friends. "Present are Agent Zaiba, Agent Poppy and one of the victims in the case, Olivia, who is assisting in the investigation. Agent Ali is..."

Where was Zaiba's little brother? Listening carefully, she could hear voices coming from the direction of the kitchen and the aroma of frying onions. "Agent Ali is cooking in the kitchen with another victim in the case, Olivia's sister Flora." Zaiba switched off the voice recorder and sighed. So much for helping with the detective work! Ali was clearly more into his cooking. Since winning the cake-baking competition at the summer fete, her little brother had expanded his skills to include savoury food too. So far he'd mastered keema matar, coriander naan, cheese straws, Yorkshire puddings and coconut rice (not all in the same meal, thank goodness!). Zaiba couldn't deny that she'd enjoyed eating all his recent kitchen experiments, Poppy *certainly* had too.

"Zaiba, over here!" Olivia waved a hand through the air. "There's a back door that leads straight to the woods."

"Perfect!" Zaiba put away the voice recorder. Olivia led them through one of the ornate reception rooms at the back of the house to a small corridor. At the end of the corridor there was a bathroom and a door leading outside with a little porch. The glass in the door's window was discoloured and spiders' webs hung in the corners of the frame. Olivia fetched the key hanging from a concealed hook in the doorframe and turned it in the lock.

"Mum and Dad couldn't work out where the key was for this door all summer. I was the one who found it by running my hand along the inside of the frame," she said proudly.

Zaiba was impressed – thinking creatively was one of the key qualities every good detective needed. "Olivia, you're going to be a massive help in this investigation!"

Olivia blushed. "Thanks, Zai. I hope so."

The three girls marched out into the woods, the light becoming dappled as they headed further among the trees.

"Try and keep an eye out for anything that looks out of place. Disturbed patches of leaves, broken branches ... that type of thing can show us if someone has been here," Zaiba instructed. "And of course, report anything that looks ... paranormal."

Poppy and Olivia exchanged worried glances but nobody turned back. Zaiba gave them an encouraging smile and went ahead into the woods. Eden Lockett's golden rule number ten: *A great leader inspires by example.*

The wood was like another world! As they got deeper inside, the trees and brambles grew more and more dense. They soon found that the path they were following disappeared and they had to climb over fallen tree stumps and bushes. This was no use! Zaiba could hardly keep track. The ground was thick with fallen leaves in red, brown and yellow. They wouldn't find any traces of ghosts or suspicious activity here – they couldn't even see the ground!

After a good five minutes of searching, Zaiba decided it was time to stop looking for clues. Olivia's smile was beginning to fade and Zaiba didn't want to spoil her afternoon. She remembered what Aunt Fouzia had told her a long time ago: "Keep your team in good spirits. Low morale can ruin an investigation." There was absolutely no point in dragging Poppy and Olivia around if they would be miserable by the end of it.

"This is no good!" she declared. She lifted her face to the sky and took a deep breath in. "Maybe we should just enjoy the afternoon, before everyone else arrives."

Poppy and Olivia agreed. This was a party, after all. They wanted to have fun! What Zaiba didn't tell them is that she would still be in detective mode, keeping her eyes focused on the ground for any clues.

But Zaiba suddenly found herself looking up at the sky at the sound of rustling leaves above her. She swivelled round and looked up at the source to see...

Poppy, dangling by her knees, above their heads!

"Look at me, I'm a monkey!" She was hanging from a sturdy oak tree branch and swinging back and forth.

Zaiba had never seen Poppy look so unsophisticated! The branch began to creak and...

"Be careful!" she cried, running to position herself underneath Poppy should she need to catch her best friend! Suddenly Poppy's skirt turned inside out and hung down over her head so that they could see all the rainbow stripes on her woollen tights. The girls burst out laughing.

"Lucky you're wearing tights, Poppy!" Olivia laughed, still doubled over in giggles.

"Otherwise we would have seen a monkey wearing pants – that'd be a first!" Zaiba added, wiping away her tears.

Poppy clambered back down the tree branch and fell against the trunk laughing. "I can't believe that happened... Right, now it's your turn!"

The girls raced through the woods searching for good trees to climb. There was a fallen elm that they used as a balancing beam to walk across a small stream. Zaiba made sure to check the base thoroughly to see whether it had fallen by mysterious means, but the rotten roots showed it was just a natural accident.

As Zaiba stood on the beam, she gazed down into the gurgling water. Her detective brain suddenly kicked into action.

"Olivia, where does this stream start?" She looked back at the distant silhouette of the manor. "It could be an access point!" The stream weaved between the trees, right up to the house. It would be easy for someone to follow *and* mask their scent and footprints!

Olivia scanned the towering trees. "I'm not sure.

Maybe there!" She pointed at a small glade in the trees. "Inside is a clearing with a little pond, Flora and I went there in our first week here when some ducklings were born."

"Ooh, cute!" Poppy clapped her hands together in excitement. "Let's go and see them."

Olivia laughed. "Yes, but ... they're ducks now."

"Oh. Still cute. Come on, let's go!"

Sure enough, as they squeezed between the trees, a clear space appeared with a deep pond in the middle. Dragonflies and pond-skaters hovered above the water and grasses sprung up in the marshy ground.

"Aha!" Zaiba beamed, picking her way over to the far side of the pond. "I knew we'd find something."

Poppy and Olivia followed carefully, trying not to slip and fall into the water. Zaiba looked closely at the ground. In the wet mud, a distinct pair of footprints could be seen.

"Do you remember in *The Haunting of Hay Hall* when Eden Lockett wanted to collect evidence of the footprints in the mud?" Zaiba asked Poppy, her eyes shining.

"Yes! She had to make a cast out of clay." Poppy looked around. "I don't think we have any of that here though."

"Luckily, nowadays we have something in our pockets that's a lot easier to carry." Zaiba took out her phone and the tape measure from her Eden Lockett backpack, which of course had a special zipped compartment just for tools. She unrolled the tape and carefully laid it across the ground, next to the footprints. "For accurate measurements," she told Olivia.

Olivia nodded. "Very important," she agreed.

Zaiba snapped several pictures for her evidence file.

"And you said that you and Flora haven't been here for a couple of weeks?" Zaiba asked, checking the measurements and recording their size in her notebook.

"That's right," Olivia confirmed. "And Mum and Dad haven't mentioned coming either. They want to finish the house before we tackle the woods."

Poppy shuddered. "A pair of ghostly footprints... Wait, do ghosts wear shoes?"

Zaiba shook her head. "I don't think so, Pops. They

usually just float."

As they stared at the footprints the air suddenly seemed chillier than before and the sky had darkened over.

"I think we should return to the house." Olivia looked back over her shoulder. "My mum will be worried if we're gone too long."

Holding hands, they slowly picked their way round in the squelchy mud. Zaiba scanned for firmer ground on the other side of the pond, but the whole area was waterlogged. There was also a large tunnel sticking out of some higher ground, with an iron grille over the top.

"What's that?" Zaiba pointed.

Olivia shrugged. "It was probably the sewage or something in the olden days."

But Zaiba wasn't so sure – along with the pair of footprints this seemed suspicious! She couldn't walk any closer to the tunnel as the ground was completely clogged up in thick mud. She wasn't sure that any of them could go through it without falling face first in a mud pie! If only she could take a closer look...

Zaiba clicked her fingers. "Got it! Pops, can you get the binoculars out of my backpack? They're in the pouch at the front."

"OK, hold still." Poppy reached forwards and managed to prise the binoculars out of the Velcro strapping, passing them over to Zaiba.

Zaiba placed them to her eyes and focused, searching to find the right spot in the trees. Then the tunnel appeared. It was definitely rusty, about the size of a slide you'd get at the park, but slightly wider and covered with iron bars. And now that she had a closer view, she could see something else attached to the grille.

"What can you see, Zai?" Poppy asked.

"Anything ... spooky?" Olivia shuddered.

"I can see something metal. A padlock!" Zaiba screwed in the end of the binoculars, which made the focus sharper. "But it looks shiny. What's a brand-new padlock doing on a rusty old sewage pipe?"

Her thoughts were interrupted by a huge rumble of thunder, which echoed across the sky, followed by a streak of white lightening that went as quickly as it came.

"Oh no! Mum said the weather would be bad today." Olivia looked up at the darkening sky. "It's going to rain."

Poppy scrunched up her nose. "That means more mud. Come on, let's get inside. I'm only a fan of mud when it's in a face mask."

Olivia was very good at remembering her way through the trees, so they were back round to the front of the house in no time.

Olivia's dad answered the door to them, cup of coffee in hand and still in his dressing gown.

"Girls! You look freezing! Come in, quick." He ushered the girls in and hung up their coats, showing them where to leave their muddy shoes by the door. "Liv, why don't you come through to the kitchen. Ali's showing us how to make –" Jack yawned and scratched his messy hair – "stuffed aloo burgers! We need all the help we can get." He plodded back into the kitchen, taking a big slurp of coffee. From the front door, the kitchen was located to the left of the foyer down a small flight of stairs.

"My dad works for a news channel, so sometimes he has to work at night," Olivia explained as they followed him down the steps into the kitchen. "I think it's just an excuse for him to have a lie-in though!"

"Hey, I heard that!" Jack called over his shoulder, plonking himself down at the big oak kitchen table and picking up a magazine.

In the middle of the room was a large, shiny marble countertop, where Ali and Flora were standing (on stools so that they could reach), chopping ingredients and mashing potatoes.

"And the most important step in cooking is hygiene," Ali was explaining to Flora and Courtney. "Did you know that on average we carry 3,200 types of bacteria from 150 different species on our hands?"

"I didn't!" Courtney mouth fell open.

"Please remove your watch, Flora. And your jewellery, Courtney," Ali instructed. "You don't want to wear those when we start shaping the burgers. They're a hiding place for bacteria."

Zaiba and Poppy rolled their eyes at each other. Ali was going a bit overboard with the germ-talk. Olivia's face had turned a distinct shade of green.

Courtney did as she was told and dropped her bracelet on the windowsill above the sink. She sighed, rubbing her wrist.

"What's wrong, darling?" Jack asked, putting down his magazine.

"I'm nervous about the party." Courtney tried to smile, but the corners of her mouth turned down. "I hope our new neighbours like us..."

Ali slapped his hand down on the counter with a startling determination.

"Courtney and Jack! With these aloo burgers, I am *sure* everyone will love you! They're stuffed with coriander and coconut and cashew nuts. What's not to like?" He looked at Olivia's mum as though she had to be out of her mind to even doubt how popular she – or his food – could be. "The only problem is, that with food this good, people won't want to ever leave!"

This put a huge smile on Courtney's face and Zaiba gave her little brother a thumbs up. People skills were a big advantage for a secret agent.

Jack was watching Flora, who had flopped against

the kitchen counter. She pushed a hand through her hair, as though mixing ingredients was hard work. "Why don't you go and explore the house a bit more, kids?" he suggested, rolling his sleeves up. "We can take over here."

"We have Hassan's top tips he emailed me this morning. I'm sure we can finish shaping the burgers," Courtney added.

Ali crinkled his forehead. "Well, if you're sure you'll be fine without my supervision..."

Jack chuckled. "We'll give you a shout if we have any problems. Go on – go and have fun." Ali opened his mouth to say something but Jack got there first. "And yes, I'll wash my hands!"

This seemed good enough for Ali, who jumped down from his stool and went to wash his hands in the sink. Flora followed suit, hanging up her apron first.

Soon enough, the whole gang were on a tour of the house led by Olivia.

Zaiba hadn't been able to look in every room on her visit yesterday. Some of the doors had been closed and it would have been rude to go inside without asking.

But now she was able to explore Oakwood Manor in all its glory!

As well as having two reception rooms, there was a games room with a pool table and a conservatory full of tropical plants and flowers. Against the gloomy sky and the patter of rain on the glass roof, the tropical blooms looked out of place.

"Look, it's me!" Poppy sang with glee, pointing at some delicate red poppies with tall green stems.

Zaiba was busy scribbling down notes in her pad and sketching out a rough map of the house as they went round. She added a small poppy sketch to the square labelled 'conservatory'.

Much to Zaiba's delight, there was a third floor of the house, which she hadn't noticed before as the staircase was hidden at the end of the west-wing corridor on the second floor. Olivia's bedroom was in the east wing so Zaiba'd had no reason to come down here.

"There are only a few rooms up here," Flora explained. "We haven't decorated them yet so they're a bit dusty."

"Are there ... spiders?" Ali's eyes widened. He still

hadn't quite managed to kick his fear after going into the secret staircase in the case of the missing diamonds.

"You're afraid of spiders but not afraid of ghosts?" Olivia asked, sounding surprised.

"Ghosts aren't real. Spiders are *very, very* real." Ali shuddered. Zaiba squeezed his hand gently. As the lead agent it was her job to make sure her team were comfortable and ready to face anything.

Olivia gently opened a creaky door to reveal a small, dimly lit room.

"What was this used for?" Zaiba wondered aloud, creeping inside slowly and taking in the objects around her.

Flora wasn't joking when she said the rooms were a bit dusty. It didn't seem like anyone had been in here for years – not even the previous owners. Dust hung in the air and coated the windows, letting through just a glimmer of light. A collection of strangely shaped, tall objects cast ghostly shadows. They looked like mannequins.

"I know what this is!" Poppy said, open-mouthed.

"Those look like the dummies fashion designers use to make their clothes on. This must have been a dressmaker's studio or something."

Zaiba gave her best friend a high five. "Great work, Poppy! And look at all these fabrics. They must be vintage by now."

There was an old wooden display cabinet with glass windows. On the shelves inside were piles and piles of fabric – some had silver threads running through them, others were covered in a riot of flowers and one of the fabrics had a print of tiny little cats! Poppy's whole face lit up. She was in fashion heaven.

"You know," she said, her nose pressed up against the glass, "a designer could create something totally incredible with some of these."

"Look here!" Ali called over, his head disappearing inside an old leather trunk. The others came over to join him.

"Mum said that one of the previous owners was an actress," Olivia said. "Maybe these are her old costumes? They're a bit faded now."

Poppy actually shrieked this time. "Costumes? Oh my gosh, I *have to* see."

The four of them crowded round the wooden trunk.

Zaiba was so engrossed that she *almost* forgot this was an investigation. *Almost*, that is, until she heard a cry and then a bang behind her.

"Help!" came Flora's muffled voice from beneath a heap of dressmaker's dummies.

"Flora!" Olivia rushed forwards. "How did that happen?"

Zaiba wasn't sure herself. One moment, the dummies had been gathered in a group in the corner, the next... How had they all suddenly toppled over on to Flora?

"Don't worry, we'll get her out." Zaiba located Flora's hand and managed to manoeuvre the dummy that was trapping her. Those things were really heavy!

"What happened?" she asked. But before a red-faced Flora could respond, another sound cut through the air, chilling Zaiba to the bone. The friends all stared at each other, wide-eyed. Then the sound came again.

It was a scream! And it was coming from downstairs.

4
A HOUSE FULL OF SECRETS

"Quick! This is an emergency!" Zaiba beckoned the group to follow her back down the stairs and towards the source of the sound. They would have to continue their investigation of the dressmaker's studio later.

They clattered down and listened to the low moaning coming from the kitchen. They ran over and burst in, to find Courtney being comforted by Jack.

Olivia ran up to her mum and gently put a hand on her back. "What happened, Mum? Are you OK?"

Courtney sobbed. "It's my silver bracelet. It's g-gone! My grandma gave it to me for my twenty-first birthday."

Jack patted her back soothingly. "We've looked

everywhere ... the sink, the drawers, the bin. Even in the burger mix! But it's just vanished."

Jack had a grim look on his face. Zaiba knew from Olivia's stories that this wasn't the first time something had disappeared without a trace at Oakwood Manor.

Olivia dragged herself over to the kitchen table and sat heavily on a stool, her head in her hands. "This is getting scary. The dressmaker's dummies going flying and now more objects going missing? This house is haunted! I wish we'd never moved here."

Tears brimmed in her eyes and Zaiba felt extremely sorry for her friend. Olivia and her family just wanted to have a nice party to meet their new neighbours and feel welcome in the neighbourhood. But all these mysterious goings-on were scaring the living daylights out of them. Even Flora, who didn't believe in ghosts, looked thoroughly miserable – and Zaiba couldn't blame her. Something was not right, and if these weren't simple accidents, and they weren't ghosts, could they be the result of something more sinister? Zaiba bit her lip, reminding herself to keep her theory a secret for now.

She didn't want to scare anyone, but it was time to take decisive action.

"Don't worry, everyone," Zaiba announced. "The Snow Leopard Detective Agency UK branch is here. We'll get to the bottom of this." She smiled reassuringly at Olivia, and Poppy gave Flora a hug. "Together we can solve this mystery. Ghost or no ghost."

Ali put his arm round Flora too, stepping up into his role of agent on duty. It seemed to work as the sisters immediately looked more hopeful.

"Do you really think you can help?" Olivia asked.

"Of course! It's what we do best!" Zaiba said, and Poppy and Ali nodded in agreement. But as she spoke, Zaiba caught Courtney's eye and couldn't help but notice – the glint of worry was still there.

"Before I take the investigation further, I'd like to know a bit more about the history of the house." Zaiba opened up her phone and tapped the voice recorder on. "Is it OK if I record our conversation?"

Jack held up his hands. He'd gone to get dressed, ready for the party. "Go ahead. Olivia has told us about your past cases. We're so grateful that you're helping out."

With the stuffed aloo burgers pressed into circles and ready for baking, Zaiba had decided to gather everyone round the kitchen table for a briefing. There'd been a lot of shady goings-on already and Zaiba thought it was important that they were all on the same page before the party guests arrived. The house was soon going to be full of people who could mess up any evidence and distract them from the mission. They could also be potential suspects and prepared to cause more trouble... Zaiba had to work fast!

"You've been such good friends to Olivia and Flora already," Courtney said, smiling at Zaiba, Poppy and Ali.

Zaiba took a deep breath. Gently, she asked, "Courtney, do you believe these incidents are ... supernatural?"

Flora and Ali immediately scoffed and Poppy threw them a warning glance.

"Sorry," Ali apologized. "But ghosts, or *jinn*, aren't real."

"Jinn?" Courtney looked confused.

Zaiba stepped in. "That's how we describe ghosts or spirits in Pakistan. They can be good or bad and come in lots of different forms, depending on what kind of supernatural creature they are. That's what Aunt Fouzia told me anyway." In Zaiba's mind, if Aunt Fouzia told her something then it must be true. She was the cleverest lady she knew, apart from Sam of course, but then the apple didn't fall too far from the tree.

"But there really is nothing to worry about, because those are all just stories," Ali countered, keeping a firm stare fixed on Zaiba. "Myths, folklore..."

"Exactly!" Flora joined in enthusiastically. "You see, from a scientific view, there's far more evidence *against* ghosts being real."

At this Jack suddenly coughed into his fist. He looked like he wanted to speak. "I have something to show you."

Getting up from the table, he went over to the large, carved oak dresser that filled one entire wall of the kitchen. He rooted round on his hands and knees in one of the lower cupboards before finally retrieving something. Zaiba thought it looked like a photo album but it was larger and stuffed full of pieces of paper.

Jack came back to his seat and thumped the item down on the table. "I've been putting together this scrapbook, to document the history of the house." He flicked through the first few pages.

Of course, a scrapbook! Zaiba made a mental note to start a scrapbook of her own for past investigations.

"At first it was mostly research about the man who built Oakwood Manor. I was thinking it might be an interesting news story. His name was Bernard Hargreaves and he designed this house alongside his daughter, Madeline Hargreaves – a talented architect in her own right. They were both very interested in ancient Egypt and the secret passageways built into the pyramids. So they decided to incorporate some of their own hidden spots in this house—"

"Hidden spots? Where?" Zaiba usually never interrupted an adult when they were speaking, but she couldn't hide her excitement any longer. *Secret passageways?* This was just like Eden Lockett's hidden staircase, or the secret tunnel in *The Haunting of Hay Hall* or... Actually, Eden Lockett had found quite a few hidden passageways in her mysteries.

"I haven't had a chance to properly check them all out yet – this really is a house full of secrets! But there's a hidden corridor behind the fireplace in the study that used to be Mr Hargreaves' personal office. Oh, and there's a murphy door." His eyes twinkled. "I'm sure you know what that is, Zaiba."

"A door hidden in a bookcase!" Zaiba's heart beat loudly in her chest. She thought Oakwood Manor might be her dream home. "What happened to the Hargreaves family?"

Jack flipped through the scrapbook and pulled out some faded black and white photographs. On inspection, Zaiba could make out the front of Oakwood Manor with what looked like soldiers sitting on chairs outside. None of them were smiling.

"The Hargreaves lived here alone until the First World War when they offered the house as a place of recovery for injured soldiers. They could come here and rest until they got their strength back."

Olivia gestured to Zaiba and Poppy. "See? That's what I heard in the village shop. Injured soldiers equal angry ghosts!"

Ali and Flora protested but Courtney told them to hush. She was enraptured in the story.

"Returning to the story..." Zaiba wanted to keep her mind on the facts. "Did they continue to live here after the war?"

Jack's face turned ashen. "Actually, during that time Mr Hargreaves died suddenly. His daughter had fallen in love with one of the soldiers. After her father died, she didn't want to live in Oakwood Manor any more as it reminded her too much of him. She moved away with her new husband and the manor fell into partial ruin. None of its inhabitants since have had enough money or time to renovate it."

"Until now," Zaiba breathed.

Jack gently closed his scrapbook and looked round at the faces who had been listening to his story in awe. "I know we don't have any evidence but I suspect that

Mr Hargreaves' spirit is still here. He's upset that the house was neglected and then bought by people outside the Hargreaves family. He's probably even angrier now that we're making some changes. He and his daughter built this house together as their family home. He thought their ancestors would live here forever..."

A hush fell over the table as Jack finished his story. Even Ali and Flora were quiet – it was a sad ending to a sad story.

Zaiba reached forwards and clicked off her voice recorder. She cleared her throat and plastered a big smile on her face. She had to lead by example and nothing would get done if they just sat and worried.

"Thank you for sharing that very useful information, Jack. If it's OK, I'd like to go and check out those hidden passageways. It's important I have a complete understanding of the layout of the house."

Courtney nodded and got up from the table, brushing down her apron, which was still covered in breadcrumbs from making the burgers.

"Of course, Zaiba. Olivia will show you around. Ali and Flora, we've got some washing-up to do!"

Ali's face dropped and Flora groaned. "But we want to go exploring too!"

Courtney put her hands on her hips. "I'm sorry, but the most important part of cooking is cleaning up afterwards!"

Grumbling, Ali and Flora got to work. Jack caught the older girls' eyes and winked, making them giggle.

Olivia quickly led Poppy and Zaiba out into the foyer. As they emerged from the small staircase, the foyer seemed even larger and more magnificent than before. Someone had rolled out an exquisite cream rug, which went perfectly with a duck-egg blue colour on the walls. Several large paintings hung on the walls and a beautiful chandelier shone in the centre of the ceiling.

The rear of the grand foyer opened up into the spacious conservatory they'd explored earlier. Zaiba noticed there was a wrought-iron spiral staircase winding up from the conservatory patio.

"Where does that staircase lead to, Olivia?" Zaiba asked. She had to add it to the map she'd sketched out in her notebook.

"There's a balcony above the outside patio that goes along the first floor. Flora and I use it for hide-and-seek!"

Zaiba approved. This house would be perfect for hide-and-seek – maybe after they finished their investigations they could have a game. But first things first... Leading off from the left and right-hand sides of the foyer were two corridors. Olivia took them down the right-hand corridor, passing a few doors on either side. As they walked, Zaiba suddenly noticed the outline of a square panel in the polished wooden floor.

"A trapdoor?" She stopped and pointed to the square. There was a small, round hole that could be used as a door handle.

"Maybe, but if it is it doesn't open." Olivia shrugged. "Here we are!" She carried on to the end of the corridor and reached the final polished oak door.

She laid a hand against the door. "This is the study. Dad uses it for his office, so it's a bit messy." She softly opened the door and the girls peered inside.

"Ooh, I love the colour scheme." Poppy sighed, taking

in the deep mahogany and bottle-green leather of the upholstery.

"And this must be the fireplace with the secret passage!" Zaiba raced forwards to inspect the ornate carved wood. There was a big wire grate covering the mouth of the fireplace for safety and the whole of the inside was thick with dust.

"We've not actually been in yet," Olivia explained. "It's probably full of mice and spiders! I'd like to have a close-up look."

Inspecting the outside of the fireplace for an obvious switch or notch in the wall, Zaiba couldn't find anything that gave away a hidden passageway. "How does it open?" She scratched her head.

Olivia smiled. "Here! There's a button in the floor under the desk."

She got down on her hands and knees and crawled under the large mahogany desk. A slightly darker panel on the floor gave away the location of the switch. She pushed down hard and with a *crack* the inside wall of the fireplace sprang open.

Poppy and Zaiba peered in, their eyes trying to adjust to the darkness. A cold draught of air slid down the chimneypiece and made them shiver.

Zaiba got out her phone torch and aimed it at the passage, but with the safety grate in the way, they could only make out some concrete walls and a lot of spiders' webs.

"Maybe we'll have more luck in the library." Zaiba straightened up and put her phone away. "Can we go there next?"

Olivia nodded. "Follow me."

The three girls trooped to the adjoining room and Zaiba found herself wishing that she lived here!

The library was gorgeous with matching polished bookcases that ran floor-to-ceiling and a number of gold gilded armchairs nestled into cosy nooks.

"This is amazing!" Poppy breathed, hoisting herself up on to one of the plump armchair cushions. "I feel like royalty."

But Zaiba couldn't focus on the armchairs or even the fact that the books were alphabetically arranged.

She pointed in awe at a shelf in her eyeline, mouth agape. Poppy followed her finger and when she saw what Zaiba was pointing at they said in unison, "A FULL COLLECTION OF EDEN LOCKETT BOOKS!"

The girls squealed and jumped up and down.

"And they're first editions!" Zaiba said, checking them over. She turned to Olivia. "Your family likes Eden Lockett? You definitely can't leave now!"

But Olivia wasn't looking at them. She was on the other side of the room, picking out books from one of the bookcases and laying them out on a little side table.

"What is it?" Zaiba asked, coming closer.

"All of these books have had letters written on their spines... I don't remember that." Olivia seemed confused but Zaiba noticed something.

She began laying the books back out in alphabetical order according to the author's surname, like in a bookshop. As she did, words began to form along the spines of the books, until a message written in blood-red ink read clearly:

STAY AWAY.

Poppy gasped and grabbed Olivia's hand. Her face had gone quite pale.

"What does it mean?" their new friend whispered.

Zaiba furrowed her brow and took a deep breath.

"Stay away from the books? Or ... stay away from the house? Either way, it doesn't make sense to me that a ghost would be writing messages on books."

"How would they even hold a pen?" Poppy agreed.

This, thankfully, made Olivia giggle.

Zaiba paced the floor, thinking. "Surely a ghost would just creep up and scare people? They don't need to leave messages. *Alive* people might do though..." She went back over to the books and examined them more closely, looking for any further clues. "We'll have to check these for fingerprints and keep them in evidence bags for further investigation."

"Fingerprints?" Olivia sounded horrified. "You think a person could be behind this? Who would leave such a horrible message?"

Zaiba looked at Olivia and tried to be as reassuring as possible. "I think that's a possibility. And the likelihood is that it's someone you know, or who knows the house, so we have to be vigilant."

Olivia nodded, putting on a brave face. "Could we keep this quiet for now? If my mum and dad find out that a person, maybe even someone we know, could be doing this, I think they'll call off the party altogether. You saw how panicked my mum was this morning."

Zaiba looked to Poppy, unsure of what to do. It would hamper the investigation to ignore this evidence but Olivia was their friend. This was quite a conundrum.

Suddenly something that she'd read scribbled in the margins of *The Haunting of Hay Hall* sprang to her mind. Slipping off her backpack she opened up her copy and flipped through the pages until she found what she was looking for. A smile crept across Zaiba's lips.

"It's a note that ammi, her birth mum, wrote years ago," Poppy explained to Olivia, who looked slightly puzzled. "What does it say, Zai?"

"The best decisions come from your heart." Zaiba thought for a moment and then snapped the book shut. "Olivia, we won't tell your parents about the evidence ...

yet! The most important thing is that your family enjoys the party and feels welcome here." *And in the meantime, she thought, we'll find out if one of the guests is behind the strange events.*

Poppy gave Zaiba a hug. "Your ammi is so smart!" Poppy was the only friend Zaiba had told properly about her birth mum. It had made them even closer as friends.

"For now, we'll put the books back in the bookcase but with the spines facing in. That way, no one will see the letters until we need to show them."

From the foyer the girls could hear Courtney calling them.

"Quick!" Zaiba whispered, and the girls got to work, carefully replacing the books on the shelves.

They'd just popped the final book back in its place when Courtney appeared in the doorway, wearing an elegant blue dress with a flash of red lipstick. She looked much happier. "There you are! I've been calling you."

Poppy ran up to Courtney and circled her, taking in every aspect of the outfit. "Oh my gosh, Courtney. You look amazing! Is that part of the new Fabrique collection?"

"It is. You sure do know your fashion, Poppy!" Courtney was impressed. "What accessories do you think I should wear?"

Zaiba and Olivia nudged each other and stifled a giggle. This was Poppy's dream – being a stylist.

"Hmmm, some statement earrings maybe? A pop of colour?" Poppy tapped her foot and pursed her lips in thought.

"A great idea, but I don't have my ears pierced." Courtney pointed to her lobes under her blond hair. Then she suddenly gave a heavy sigh.

"Don't be sad! What about a necklace?" Poppy suggested.

"Thank you, Poppy, but I'm not worried about that. It's this party." Courtney sat down on one of the armchairs and the girls came to gather round her. Zaiba thought that on the ornate chair in her elegant cocktail dress, Courtney really did look like a queen.

"I do hope nothing *strange* happens. I wouldn't want the neighbours to get the wrong idea of us."

Zaiba came to sit in front of Courtney and smiled

encouragingly. "Don't worry, Courtney. Nothing will go wrong. You have us here, remember?"

At that moment the grandfather clock in the corner of the library rang ominously.

Bong bong bong bong bong.

It was 5 p.m. already!

"My goodness, you girls had better go get ready for the party!" Courtney got up and ushered them out of the room. "The guests will be arriving soon. I've still got to put those burgers in the oven."

The girls, joined by Ali and Flora, headed upstairs to get changed. But just before Zaiba turned the corner on the landing she looked down and gave Courtney a reassuring smile.

Olivia and Flora's mum smiled back. "Thank you!" she mouthed at Zaiba, giving her a warm feeling in her tummy. The party would be a success, Zaiba was sure of it. Absolutely sure.

5
LET'S GET THIS PARTY STARTED

"This is Agent Zaiba and the time is 18:00 hours. Initial investigation of the house is complete. We have discovered a secret fireplace but were unable to access. We also found a mysterious message in the library. This seems unlikely to have been the work of a ghost, so—"

There was a light tapping on the door of the bathroom where Zaiba was getting ready and she quickly clicked off her voice recorder.

"Zaiba, are you done? I need to use the mirror!" It was Poppy.

"Just a minute." Zaiba had been combing her hair before she'd been distracted by her detective's log.

For the party she'd decided to plait it into two braids and she'd tied a little white flower at the end of each bobble, at Poppy's suggestion.

"All done!" Zaiba opened the door and jokingly flipped her plaits at Poppy.

"They look great!" Her best friend admired her braids. "Maybe I should change my hair..."

Olivia groaned from the bedroom. "You've already changed it twice! Just pop it in a ponytail." Zaiba joined Olivia back in the bedroom while Poppy fussed with her hair in the bathroom mirror. The house was so big that each bedroom had its own bathroom attached.

Olivia had opted for a pair of high-waisted trousers with a cool striped shirt. She'd put her curly red hair up into a pretty, messy bun. Zaiba approved of Olivia's sharp dress sense – she must have got it from her mum!

She turned to Zaiba, suddenly very serious. "Zaiba, whatever you do – don't laugh when you see Flora and Ali."

Zaiba was concerned. "What? Why?" But her questions were quickly answered when Ali and Flora

bounded in, both dressed as tiny waiters in white shirts complete with a bow tie. Zaiba bit her lip to stop from laughing out loud.

"Isn't it great?" Ali straightened out his shirtsleeves. "We got the bow ties from Jack!"

"Since Mum said we're helping to hand out drinks, we thought we should dress the part. That way we'll blend in more when we're gathering evidence, you know – undercover," Flora added seriously.

Zaiba nodded vigorously. Luckily, she was saved by the chiming of the doorbell. The first guests were arriving!

"Yay, party guests!" Poppy squealed, dashing out of the bathroom and out on to the landing. As she caught sight of Ali and Flora she added a quick, "Cute costumes, you two!"

Ali grumbled. "They aren't costumes, they're our uniforms!"

Zaiba laughed. "Come on, we have to meet the guests."

As Poppy had told Zaiba many times, you should

always turn up to a party "fashionably late". Apparently their parents hadn't got the memo, as they were the first to arrive. Hassan had opted for one of his more casual kurtas in navy blue and Zaiba was relieved he hadn't gone for the beaded, embroidered gold number he sometimes pulled out of the wardrobe. Jessica was in a typical arty outfit, a floaty dress in lots of different shades of blue with a matching shawl. After Courtney and Jack had greeted them, Zaiba ran up to her mum and dad, giving them a hug, before moving on to give Poppy's mum Emma a big hug too.

"How was the netball match, Mum?" Poppy asked, retying the scarf around her mum's neck at a jauntier angle. She'd told Zaiba earlier that she'd picked out the white blouse and dark green trousers so that the colours would 'complement' Poppy's own outfit.

"It was brill, sweetie!" Emma's strawberry-blond bob bounced as she spoke. "I'm so excited for the party now!"

"Us too," Jessica added.

"I can't wait for dinner." Hassan rubbed his stomach as he looked around. This made Courtney and Jack laugh.

73

Good, Zaiba thought, *maybe they'll feel less nervous now that some guests are actually here.*

"Where's Bean tonight?" Zaiba asked Emma. Bean was Poppy's dog. He was a whippet and Emma's pride and joy!

"Oh, she's at Nan's house, probably getting spoiled rotten," Poppy answered. (They'd thought about letting Bean join the Snow Leopard Detective Agency as a sidekick, but she got way too distracted by interesting smells and squirrels!)

"Darling, are you sure you want to carry that backpack around?" Jessica asked, looking at Zaiba's combination outfit of shiny shalwar kameez and Eden Lockett backpack. Hassan laughed and looked at his daughter lovingly.

"A party dress and a utility backpack ... that's my daughter!" he chuckled.

"Here, Ali," Zaiba whispered to her brother, slipping off the backpack. "Can you stow this under the biggest sofa in the living room for me?"

Ali nodded subtly and together with Flora, the mini-waiters escorted the parents into the largest reception room for their welcome drinks. Almost on cue, the doorbell rang again.

Courtney answered it and was greeted by their nearest neighbours, the Freemans. Zaiba noticed that they didn't look exactly in the mood for a party. Both adults had very sour expressions, like they'd just smelled something unpleasant. Instead of party outfits Zaiba thought they looked better suited for a business meeting. The woman wore a black dress with sharp shoulders, though she had put on extremely sparkly diamond earrings and a matching necklace. The man was wearing a simple black suit. He had a very neat beard and moustache.

Zaiba and Poppy quickly squeezed each other's hands in warning. They knew the Freemans. Their son, Ade, was hiding sulkily behind his parents. He was in the year below them at school and known for being a show-off. He looked uncomfortable in his crisp white shirt and black trousers and his shoes looked almost as shiny as his mum's earrings. His curly black hair had been smartly braided back for the occasion. Zaiba concluded that these were serious people from their formal clothing, but that they wanted to impress – hence the expensive jewellery.

"Hello, Courtney. Thank you for inviting us. I'm Sefi."
Ade's mum stuck her hand out and shook Courtney's stiffly.

"I'm Max." His dad followed suit with the hand shaking.
"It's a shame you couldn't clear those pine trees in the
driveway, they shed terribly in the autumn."

"Oh, uh, yes, I suppose they do..." Courtney stammered.

"Would you like to join our parents in the reception
room?" Zaiba stepped forwards, beckoning Poppy and
Olivia to follow her.

"Yes, there are some drinks and snacks in there if you'd
like," Olivia added, showing them the way.

"You come too, Ade." Poppy steered the sulky boy in the
direction of the reception room. He'd fished his phone out
of his trouser pocket and was busily tapping away on the
screen, avoiding eye contact with everyone.

"I hope there are meat-free options, I did mention well
in advance that I'm vegetarian." Sefi shot a stern look at
Courtney over her shoulder before she disappeared into
the lounge.

"Ignore them and don't worry," Zaiba whispered to

Courtney. "I'll keep them occupied."

Courtney squeezed her shoulder and headed back into the kitchen to check on the food.

In the living room, Jack was doing his best to dodge Max and Sefi's jibes, while Ali and Flora kept everyone's drinks topped up. There was soft jazz music playing in the background and Courtney had decorated the room tastefully with beautiful bouquets of flowers and pretty fairy lights. It helped the eerie emptiness of the house slip away.

Beside her, Ade took a sip of his soft drink and made a face. "Eurgh, is this squash? We only have cordials at our house."

"Well, you aren't at your house, so have some manners," Zaiba said in a low voice. Luckily before Ade could complain, some new guests joined the room and he went back to playing on his phone instead.

"This is Isabela and Anita," Courtney announced. "They're our neighbours – they brought round a delicious cake when we moved in!" The doorbell rang again and Courtney excused herself once more.

"Hi, lovely to meet you!" Hassan said, breaking the silence.

"Nice to meet you too," Anita smiled back, holding Isabela's hand firmly. Then quietly she added to Isabela, "Would you like to sit down, darling?"

Isabela nodded and the two women sat down on the sofa. The other guests got back to chatting and Zaiba took note of this strange behaviour. Isabela didn't seem unfriendly, just *unwell* perhaps?

The sky was dark now and the curtains had been left open, revealing trees swaying violently in the wind. Their branches cast moving shadows over the room and Zaiba secretly thought that the old manor was a *little* bit creepy.

Next to arrive was a middle-aged man with a small girl. Jack introduced them as Jay, the previous owner of the house and his daughter, Layla. Zaiba's ears pricked up and she gestured to Ali to go and offer Jay a glass of water. The previous owner of the house would certainly know a lot about its history, and perhaps something about the spooky goings-on.

He could be very useful! Zaiba thought.

She scanned the room for her co-agents. Olivia was doing her best to chat to Ade, who was still showing off about all the things he had in *his* house. Poppy was acting as backup, trying to stop Max and Sefi from being *too* rude to Courtney.

Zaiba felt a tugging at her sleeve and looked down to see the girl Jack had introduced a moment earlier, staring at her with wide eyes.

"Hi, I'm Layla! I'm six!" the girl beamed up at Zaiba.

"Nice to meet you, Layla." Zaiba smiled back. "But I'm actually concentrating on something at the moment—"

"I used to live here!" Layla said excitedly.

Of course. Zaiba chided herself for not taking the girl more seriously. Layla could be a real help to the investigation. All of these witnesses to the history of the house! This couldn't be more perfect. This would also give Zaiba the chance to check out any secret spots in the house – places that were perfect for a suspect to sneak through.

"That must have been exciting – did you have any

favourite hiding places? Or a special place you liked to play?" Zaiba asked.

"Like the magic bookcase you mean?" Layla's eyes lit up. "I can show you!"

Zaiba would have taken her up on the offer there and then, had the last two guests not arrived at that moment.

"Can you show me later? Is that OK?" Zaiba asked.

Layla nodded, her little black pigtails bobbing, and gave Zaiba a hug. She really was a cute little girl.

"Ah, Laurence!" Jack said, stretching his arms out to the final guest. "I didn't hear you ring the bell! Oh, and Alexandra is here too."

Laurence, grey-haired and dressed in a sharply tailored suit and shiny shoes, shook Jack's hand. "Don't worry, I actually came to the back door, I'm so used to going that way from doing all the house viewings."

"Laurence was our estate agent," Jack explained to the group. "He helped us buy the house."

"We know," Max replied coolly, sharing a pointed look with Sefi.

"I spotted Laurence heading to the back entrance so I just followed him. Sorry for the confusion." Alexandra, the woman who had arrived at the same time as Laurence, explained.

"Oh, forgive me, this is Alexandra," Jack said. "She's a new friend and a property developer in the surrounding areas. We met at the gym, actually."

"Well, that explains how she beat me to the back door then!" Laurence guffawed loudly and slapped Jack on the back. "I'm getting quite slow these days."

Zaiba looked hard at Alexandra, trying to get a read on her. She looked about the same age as Jessica, tall and slender, but her face was a lot less friendly. Her brown eyes had a hard stare and a blunt-cut fringe made her expression seem perpetually angry. Zaiba noted all these features in detail – a good memory was an important part of being a detective. Eden Lockett's golden rule number fifteen: *Take note of everything around you. The smallest detail could be the biggest clue.* Grabbing a napkin and a pen, she jotted down all the guests.

Mum and Dad

Emma (Poppy's mum)

Neighbours Sefi and Max, Ade (their son) – all very rude!

Neighbours Anita and Isabela – Isabela acting strange

Jay, Layla (his daughter) – used to live here

Laurence – estate agent

Alexandra – something to do with property?

Zaiba took a deep breath. That was a lot of new faces to keep an eye on. She folded up the napkin and tucked it away in her pocket, ready to copy into her notebook later.

Scanning the room, Zaiba decided to introduce herself and get a closer look at the newest arrivals. She passed by Poppy and Olivia quietly whispering, "Follow me!" Then she made her way over to the adults. Alexandra and Laurence were politely chatting about something called a 'housing market' and the difficulties of finding land for new 'developments'. Zaiba felt her eyes widen and a yawn stretch across her lips. *Wow, adult conversations are boring.* She made a mental note to remember to always stay fun.

"Excuse me, would you like us to take your coats?" Zaiba asked politely, during a gap in their conversation.

"Oh, yes please." Alexandra took off her heavy coat, scarf and gloves. Laurence hadn't brought a coat and was only wearing gloves and a striped blue scarf despite it being quite chilly outside.

"It's about time you offered," Sefi said haughtily, dropping her coat into Poppy's hands.

"This needs to be hung up carefully," Max told Olivia, who had taken his jacket.

The children, including Flora and Ali, took all the assembled clothing down to the kitchen where there was a row of big brass hooks for hanging coats up.

"That Max and Sefi are so rude!" Flora complained. "He even told me that his wine wasn't chilled enough, even though this red wine should be served between sixteen to eighteen degrees Celsius. I checked with Mum."

"That's between sixty-one and sixty-five degrees Fahrenheit," Ali added, as if it would help Zaiba understand.

"Just keep your cool, everyone, we have to stay alert," Zaiba warned them, hanging up Sefi's coat.

Poppy laid Laurence's gloves on the side table, not without noting their designer label of course. "Giuseppe Fi. Very nice."

"Nicer than this scarf," Olivia replied, hanging Alexandra's drab grey woollen scarf on a peg. "It's got paint splashes all over it."

"Honestly, don't people know to dress for a party?" Poppy rolled her eyes.

"If Alexandra likes painting, she should talk to Mum about it," Ali said to Zaiba and she nodded. Jessica was an art teacher and a keen painter too.

"Right, Zaiba. Everyone's here." Poppy turned to her best friend and put her hands on her hips. "What's our next move?"

The group huddled closer and looked intently at Zaiba. The house was suddenly full of people who knew all about Oakwood Grange. It was so obvious!

"We need to find out how much each guest knows about the house," she said quickly. "See if the previous owners noticed anything spooky going on. But remember!" She glanced around her friends, giving the secret sign for secrecy – which was a zip along the lips. "Don't give too much away! After all … one of these guests could be a suspect. We just need to find out their motives."

Eyes widened, then the group nodded eagerly, zipping their own lips in unison.

"Do you really think we can solve this?" Olivia asked, hope lighting up her face. "It would make Mum and Dad so happy."

Zaiba smiled. "I don't *think* we can. I *know* we can." She raised a hand for a high five, as the sounds of the party grew louder. Everyone seemed to be having a great time – it was the perfect cover for their investigation. "Right, team, let's get to work!"

6
THINGS THAT GO BUMP IN THE DARK

The drinks were flowing, the music playing and all the guests chatting happily. To the untrained eye, the party was going perfectly. But Zaiba wasn't untrained. In fact, staying alert when everything was running smoothly was an important skill for a secret agent. Who knew when danger was lurking round the corner?

Zaiba kept her eyes peeled as she scanned the room, watching the grown-ups nattering away and observing their body language. Did anyone seem guarded, crossing their arms? Or suspicious, shifting their weight from foot to foot? She'd learned this tip from her aunt Fouzia – body language was 'the secret language of humans'.

So far the most suspicious activity was her dad sneaking yet another stuffed aloo burger on to his plate along with a handful of crisps despite Jessica trying to keep Hassan on a healthy-eating plan.

"I suppose parties don't count as healthy-eating days," Ali giggled to Zaiba, following her gaze. He and Flora had given up on topping up glasses and clearing empty plates and now they went to lounge on the sofa. So much for being professional waiters! Poppy and Olivia were helping themselves to the buffet Courtney had laid out. Zaiba was tempted herself by the chicken wings, the pomegranate salad and warm, crusty bread rolls. But she didn't want to drop her guard even for one moment. Poppy must have noticed her staring because she popped over with a plate, topped with a little bit of everything from the buffet.

"Even secret agents have to eat, you know." She winked at Zaiba and gave her a smile.

"You're the best, Pops," Zaiba said through a mouthful of salad. Poppy headed back to Olivia to discuss the difference between using maple syrup and honey in a glaze. It seemed that Poppy had found someone who shared her love for food!

A high tinkling sound caught everyone's attention and the group turned to look at Courtney, who was lightly tapping a fork against her glass.

"Hi, everyone!" She looked round the room, beaming. All her nerves were forgotten – for now. "Jack and I just wanted to say again, how lovely it is to have you all here. It can be quite daunting moving to a small town where everyone knows each other." Her cheeks flushed. "We're looking forward to getting to know you!"

Zaiba felt her own cheeks flushing. She knew exactly how it felt, when you weren't always sure if people would open themselves up to you. She thought back to the first time the Snow Leopard Detective Agency UK branch had shared their crime theory with an audience of grown-ups. She'd felt so nervous at the time! Thankfully, Zaiba's theory had been watertight and everyone had believed them. Zaiba had had to draw on all her inner strength, but she hadn't looked back since. She felt certain that it could be the same for Courtney, if only she could have faith in herself.

"Yes!" Jack joined in. "If you'll have us," he added with a tense laugh. Thankfully, there were a few chortles in response from the crowd.

Jack raised his glass in a toast. "To the—"

Snap! Before he could finish, the room was plunged into darkness.

Zaiba went into instant alert mode. She scanned the ceiling and its ancient chandeliers – she remembered that their wiring was probably as old as they were.

"What's happened?" Zaiba heard a panicked voice from the corner of the dark room.

"A faulty light maybe?" She recognized her dad's voice.

"So sorry, everyone!" There was a definite edge to Courtney's voice. "Oh dear, it must be a power cut. If we just wait a moment ... I'm sure the lights will come back on." But Courtney didn't seem very certain, her voice wobbling at the end of her sentence. The crowd of guests waited in silence for what felt like the longest minute of Zaiba's life.

"Maybe we should play 'murder in the dark' like when we had sleepovers as children?" Emma laughed, trying to break the tension.

But a deafening SMASH from the window broke it instead.

There was a collective gasp and chilling scream that Zaiba recognized instantly as Courtney's.

Oh no! Zaiba thought. *Another ghostly attack? It couldn't be.*

In the small amount of moonlight that filtered through the smashed window, Zaiba could just make out a solid rectangular-shaped object on the floor.

"Someone get the lights back on!" Zaiba called, as she raced towards Courtney and Jack. She grabbed her backpack that Ali had stowed beneath the sofa and fished out the torch.

"I think I remember where the fuse box is," Laurence offered. *He does know the house,* Zaiba thought. *Perhaps a little too well?* He strode out of the room with purpose.

Zaiba, Olivia and Flora gathered round Jack who was kneeling on the floor beside an oblong orange brick.

"Ali, collect this as evidence," Zaiba said, neatly stepping in front of Jack before he could contaminate it with his fingerprints. "There are some clear bags in my backpack." Zaiba could feel herself in full agent mode now. She felt Ali rummaging in her backpack as it hung from her shoulders. It was difficult in the dark but eventually he found the evidence bags.

"So, carrots don't actually help you to see in the dark!" he exclaimed over her shoulder. "I should have known it wasn't true!"

"Not now, Ali," Zaiba groaned.

"Daddy, you're bleeding!" Flora gasped in horror. With Zaiba's torch on, there was now enough light to see the broken glass strewn on the floor and Jack's scratched hands.

"I must have fallen in the broken glass..." Jack murmured, searching for something to stop the bleeding.

Zaiba glanced out into the connecting hallway to see how Laurence was doing with finding the fuse box. They needed more light in here – and quickly!

But what she saw instead was a shadowy figure, sneaking round near the back door and making their way towards the main foyer. Was it Laurence? Or something much less *human*?

"I need to follow a lead," she said quickly. "Poppy, take over here." Zaiba scrambled up and rushed out into the hallway, hoping to catch the mysterious presence before it got away. But in the dark, it was impossible to make out any shapes in the corridor. There wasn't even enough light to cast any shadows.

A low humming sound started, like a generator powering on. Bulbs flickered into life. Zaiba blinked in the light. Laurence must have finally located the fuse box – and now there was ... no sign of anything at all. Not a single person in the corridor, not even a ghost. But before Zaiba could turn back, shoulders slumped, there came another cry.

"Oh no!"

She cocked her head on one side, listening carefully. The shout of despair came from the living room – definitely the living room. *What now?*

Zaiba raced over, minding the bits of broken glass on the floor. She found Sefi wailing on her knees, gingerly picking up shards of coloured glass. "The beautiful stained glass. It's ruined!"

Ade seemed a bit embarrassed by his mum. Zaiba felt her mind buzzing. Why did Sefi care so much that the glass was broken?

"Excuse me," Zaiba said politely. There was never any reason not to be polite – especially around grown-ups.

Sefi sat back on her heels. "Yes?"

"Would you mind not touching the glass yet?"

Sefi frowned. "What do you mean?"

Zaiba pointed out the pattern the broken glass made on the floor. "Well, you see, the way the glass has landed could help us work out where the culprit was standing when they threw the brick."

Sefi stared at the floor. "You're right!" The shards of glass had sprayed out in a column of sparkling pieces, and if you followed the column back towards the broken window and out across the garden, Zaiba could get an idea of where the brick was thrown from.

Sefi got to her feet and stared down at the glass. "Can we just be sure to keep all the pieces? They're a part of history!"

"Of course!" Zaiba said. Maybe the house's past could be pieced back together, once this investigation was over.

"They must have been standing behind that yew tree!" Flora had come to stand beside Zaiba, and pointed with a trembling finger. Then she grabbed Zaiba's arm. "Oh, you're so clever, Zaiba!"

Zaiba gave a modest smile. "A detective is only as clever as the clues allow her to be."

But Flora wasn't having any of it. "I think you're a genius!" she said, her eyes wide.

Zaiba was secretly pleased but was about to argue that 'genius' was a bit of a stretch – expert maybe – when suddenly she remembered that there were more important things at hand. Jack was still bleeding and poor Courtney had had to go and sit down on an armchair with Poppy's mum comforting her.

"Do you think someone should go and find whoever's out there?" Jack asked no one in particular, looking up from his bleeding hands.

There was no response. It didn't seem like anyone was up for stalking through the dark woods.

"I don't think that's a good idea," Isabela piped up for the first time that evening. Zaiba hadn't even noticed her in the room until now. "It could be dangerous and someone has already got hurt."

Anita stood closer to Isabela, as if she was trying to protect her. Zaiba agreed, no one should go out into the woods now. Eden Lockett's golden rule number five: *A good agent always ensures the safety of her friends.*

Speaking of which...

Zaiba looked over to where Poppy was doing her best to clean Jack's wounds with a wet cloth, but it was obvious that his hands needed to be bandaged. Ali was making a show of helping but Zaiba could see that he was keeping his eyes fixed firmly away from the wounds. He wasn't the biggest fan of blood. Luckily Hassan stepped in and took the first-aid kit from Poppy.

He turned to Zaiba. "I'll take care of this." He made a shoo-ing motion with his hands. "What we really need now is a detective..."

"Thanks, Dad." Zaiba's heart swelled. She reached up on tiptoe to whisper in his ear. "Would you mind photographing the broken glass before it's cleared up?"

Hassan angled his phone out of his pocket and winked. He hadn't been too keen on Zaiba's detective work to start with, after what had happened to her ammi. But now he fully supported her, after seeing how good she'd been at solving past mysteries. She was going to make him, Aunt Fouzia and her ammi proud!

"Agents, assemble!" Zaiba called, quickly heading out into the corridor and towards the back door.

Poppy and Ali joined her immediately – the Snow Leopard Detective Agency UK did *not* hang around.

"Emergency meeting," Zaiba explained, tipping everything in her backpack on to the floor. "When the lights were off, I spotted someone, or something, out here. He, she or IT," she gulped, "came from the back door – the one we used earlier."

"Any idea who it was?" Poppy asked.

"Nope, but this might help." Zaiba produced her DIY

fingerprint-taking set from the backpack and handed it to Ali. "Here. This is your speciality."

Ali smiled proudly. "It would be my pleasure!"

He immediately set to work on the back door, dusting it with the fine black powder included in the set. Carefully and precisely he blew off the excess dust and pressed down in several places with clear tape. He was concentrating so hard that his glasses had slipped to the end of his nose, making him look like a little scientist. Zaiba and Poppy watched Ali work, transfixed, as he used a magnifying glass to identify seven different sets of prints. They stuck the tape down on a plain piece of paper for further identification later.

Zaiba snapped a couple of pictures of the brick, but there was nothing out of the ordinary about it. It was just, well, a brick. Ali tried to dust it with the fine powder but he couldn't pick up any fingerprints.

"Either there aren't any prints," he explained, "or the larger pores in the brick are letting the dust particles fall through."

Zaiba sighed. They'd have to save the brick to be

tested when they had access to better equipment.

The sound of a fork chiming on glass rang again, but this time Courtney wasn't about to propose a toast to her new neighbours.

Zaiba, Poppy and Ali packed up their equipment and made it back to the living room just in time for the announcement.

"I wanted to inform you all that the police have been called," Courtney said gravely. "As I'm sure you're aware this is a *very* serious matter and they've told me –" she glanced around at her guests – "that NO ONE is to leave the house until they arrive."

There was an audible intake of breath. Zaiba found her mind whirring as the various grown-ups shared panicked glances and whispered to each other.

"I only came for the mushroom canapes!" she heard someone say.

"I wanted to get back to watch the darts!" hissed another, sinking on to a chair.

Were these people Courtney's guests or had they just become her ... prisoners? The mood of this party was changing fast.

Jack held up his freshly bandaged hands as he joined his wife. "I suggest that while we wait for the police, we continue the party as best we can." He looked around the room with a hopeful grin. "After all, there are still plenty of those tasty aloo burgers left!" Zaiba noticed her brother beam with pride. "As much as I want to, I certainly can't eat them all myself."

There was a small nervous chuckle from the group — everyone was on edge now. Although they tried to go back to normal, chatting and swapping stories, it was hard to forget the dramatic events that had just happened. Hassan managed to find a pack of cards on a dresser and suggested a game of Go Fish, but the small group he managed to gather looked extremely awkward, sitting stiffly in a circle as he went over the rules.

Zaiba shook her head. If they were going to wait for the local police to solve this, they'd be waiting a long time! The police chief was well meaning, but as Zaiba had witnessed at the summer fete, he wasn't the sharpest tool in the box. He'd once tried to launch an investigation into a handbag-stealing gang that never existed! If this situation was left to him, the police chief would arrest the entirely wrong person, with the wrong motive, for the wrong crime.

No. Zaiba knew she *had* to solve this mystery before he arrived on the scene. This was it. They were up against the clock. She located Ali and Poppy who had gone to survey the damage of the broken glass and headed over there, dodging past Alexandra and Laurence having a heightened conversation about business, *yet again*.

Alexandra seemed sad and Zaiba just caught a snippet of what she was saying as she went past, something about 'losing a deal'? She'd have to follow up on that later. For now, she had her sights set on the rest of her team.

"Poppy, Ali," Zaiba said in a low voice once she'd reached them, "we have a deadline to figure this out by. I'm making you both deputy head agents on this – we're going to have to split up to work faster."

Poppy and Ali nodded sharply.

"Ali, I need you and Flora to work on more

fingerprinting – we need to find out who used the back door. We need all the evidence we can find. Go find Flora and then report back to me."

"Right!" Ali shot off in search of Flora.

"Pops, I need you to work your charm interviewing the adults with Olivia. Can you go find her for me?"

"I'm on it! What are you going to do, Zai?"

"I'm going to round up Layla and Ade, to see what they know, and to explore. There must be more evidence around the house of someone sneaking about."

Poppy made a face. "Ade, really? But he's *so* annoying."

Zaiba put a hand on Poppy's shoulder. "We have to be professional, and we need all the help we can get."

Poppy sighed. "You're right. OK, I'll go and get Olivia. Text me your location."

The two girls high-fived and Zaiba went off in the opposite direction to round up her recruits.

She found Ade sulking on a stool in the corridor, playing a noisy game on his phone. He seemed surprised when she asked him to help out with the investigation.

"Well ... I guess it will be better than hanging around,

listening to your parents' boring conversations." He put his phone away.

Charming.

Luckily they didn't have to look far for Layla. She was stuck to her dad's side like a limpet, holding his hand. The dramatic event must have frightened her.

"Hi, Layla," Zaiba said sweetly. "I was wondering if you wanted to come and play with us. You could show us your favourite spots in the house?"

Jay's face lit up and he gently wiggled Layla's hand in his own. "That sounds fun, Layla. Why don't you go with Zaiba?" He seemed relieved to have something to take his daughter's mind off the smashed window.

Layla nodded eagerly and immediately let go of her dad's hand to take Zaiba's instead. "Come with me! I'll take you to my playroom!"

Ade and Zaiba followed Layla as she swept out into the foyer, up the stairs and across the west-wing corridor. She was fast as a rocket!

"Here we are!" She stopped in front of a plain brown door, much shorter than the rest in the corridor, with a piece of rope where the handle should be.

"Uh, Layla, you said this was a playroom." Ade rolled his eyes, panting slightly. "It looks more like a store cupboard to me."

Layla pouted and pulled on the piece of rope. With a firm tug, the door swung open and—

"Wow!" Zaiba couldn't believe her eyes.

Inside was a tall thin room, stocked with stationery, two desks, corkboards, whiteboards, tape, coloured pens – everything you could need to conduct a proper crime-scene investigation. It was like her desk at home but even better!

They walked in and Ade looked around him, unimpressed. "It looks like Mrs Booker uses this as her study. My mum's office at home is a *lot* bigger than this."

But Zaiba wasn't bothered whether Ade was impressed or not. She immediately whipped out her phone and sent a message to the Snow Leopard Detective Agency group chat.

In Courtney's study on first floor. Come quickly. Think we've found our HQ for this investigation!

7
CRIME SCENE HQ

The door thudded shut with a definite *whack*. The
small study was now crammed with Zaiba, Poppy,
Ali, Olivia, Flora, Ade *and* Layla all inside. The air was
still and Zaiba noticed that the sound of downstairs
was completely muffled by the closed door and
thick carpet. It was silent. Before, Zaiba might have
found this spooky but as the night drew on, she was
becoming more convinced that a ghost wasn't behind
the mysterious incidents. There was an explanation for
all the strange goings-on – she just needed to find out
what it was.

Zaiba cleared her throat. "Thanks for meeting me

here so quickly," she began, gazing round at the faces watching her. "As you all know, the police have been informed of the incident, so we have to act quickly to solve the mystery before they arrive and interfere. To start with, it would be good to know where everyone was when the lights went off. If we all work together we should be able to accurately place each guest on this map I've drawn."

Zaiba gestured to the big whiteboard behind her where she'd outlined the perimeters of the reception room, including the two entrances, the smashed window and the tables.

"I've made these name markers from Post-it notes, so we can stick them on to the map." Zaiba produced nineteen Post-it notes in a variety of colours, each marked with the names of a guest at the party. After five minutes of *umm*-ing and *ahh*-ing, including a few instances of raised voices, the group had managed to place eighteen of the stickers on the board in agreement.

Zaiba stood back to take it all in.

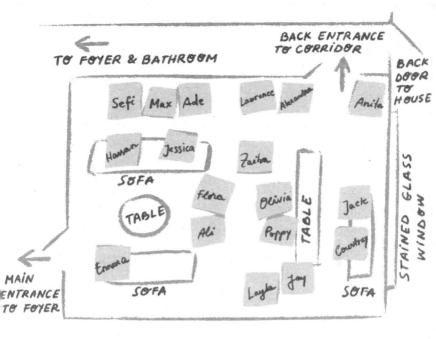

"And we're one hundred per cent sure that the only person who wasn't in the room was Isabela?" Poppy tapped her foot against the floor, deep in thought.

"Yes, we've said that a thousand times!" Ade was getting hot and flustered in the small room, and Zaiba could see sweat beads forming on his forehead. Clearly not everyone had the patience for detective work, which was a shame as Zaiba hated leaving people out.

"So, if Isabela was the only person who wasn't around when the lights went off, then it must have been her who cut the power!" Olivia said to Zaiba.

"And threw the brick through the window!" Flora added.

Zaiba held her hand up. "Hold on. You can't just blame a crime on someone based on one piece of circumstantial evidence." Zaiba had learned that term from her favourite court-based TV show at the moment, *Judge Janet*.

"What's circus-stantal?" Layla asked in a small voice. She hadn't left Zaiba's side the whole time they'd been in the room.

"Oh, sorry, Layla. It means that the evidence doesn't directly prove that Isabela is guilty. After all, there could be another reason why she left the room."

"I wish I had an encyclopedia here," Ali murmured, unhappy at a gap in his own knowledge.

"You can borrow mine later," Flora whispered to him.

Zaiba thought this might be a bit confusing for the group to understand. It had taken Zaiba at least six episodes *and* asking Aunt Fouzia to understand herself!

"How about this," she offered. "We should list down

all the strange things that have happened up until tonight and any pieces of evidence we have found. It will help to clear things in our heads. Poppy, can you write while I speak?"

Poppy nodded and picked up a piece of chalk, ready to take notes.

- BROKEN VASE IN FOYER
- PLATES SMASHED IN KITCHEN
- FURNITURE MOVED AROUND
- FOOTPRINTS IN THE MUD
- COURTNEY'S BRACELET GONE MISSING
- DRESSMAKER'S DUMMIES SUDDENLY FALLING OVER
- PAINTED LETTERS ON BOOKS IN THE LIBRARY
- LIGHTS BEING CUT
- BRICK THROWN THROUGH WINDOW

Ade whistled, not looking up from fiddling on his phone. "Wow, that's a lot of creepy stuff. Why do you live here again?"

Poppy shot him a stern look and thankfully he shut up.

Zaiba examined the list once again and thought carefully. *What would their next move be?* Now that it was laid out in front of her, she knew the time for planning was over. Action is what they needed now – before any more strange things happened!

Whipping out her phone, she clicked on the voice recorder once more. "This is Agent Zaiba reporting from the crime-scene headquarters." Ali looked up and pulled a face, but Zaiba turned her back on him to continue talking into the phone. "After a planning meeting, the team will now split up to investigate in different areas of the house. Poppy and Olivia will commence their interviews with the guests." Zaiba covered the mouthpiece and added to Poppy, "Try to be subtle, don't make anyone suspicious." She spoke into the voice recorder again. "Ali and Flora will be stationed in the kitchen preparing dessert. This gives them the perfect opportunity to begin testing fingerprints. Olivia will bring them glasses from the guests to compare prints to the ones found on the back door."

"Brilliant, a lab!" Ali and Flora high-fived.

"Great plan, Zai." Poppy patted her on the back.

"Uhhhhh and what exactly do you need us for?" Ade moaned, pointing to himself and Layla.

Zaiba smiled down at her new little friend. "Layla is going to show us some of the secret places in the house. I need your help, Ade, as some of the entrances are quite heavy and stiff to open."

Ade drew himself up tall. "Well, I am very strong so I can *definitely* help with that."

Poppy was behind him so he didn't see when she did the most dramatic eye-roll of all time, but she did make Layla giggle.

Zaiba clapped her hands together and beamed at her group of detectives. This plan was really coming together. "Right, team. Let's get to work!"

8
TERRIFYING TUNNELS AND BOTTOMLESS BASEMENTS

"Slow down, Layla!" Zaiba called, panting as she chased the little girl round the twists and turns of Oakwood Manor. Fortunately it was so huge that they didn't have to pass the room where the adults were. Besides, if they did, all they would see was Layla running past the door like a streak of lightning, with Zaiba and Ade behind. It looked more like a game of chase then an investigation!

Behind her, Zaiba could hear Ade huffing and puffing. A few times, he fell out of sight and Zaiba was worried he would get lost. The house was like a maze with the amount of corridors and passageways. If it wasn't for Layla, Zaiba might well have lost her way herself. But Ade always seemed to find them – it was almost as if he knew where he was going.

"And here's another hidey-hole where I used to store my favourite toys," Layla chattered on, dropping to her hands and knees to slide open a panel in the wall of one of the guest bedrooms. This was the third sliding panel she'd shown them! Mr Hargreaves was definitely a fan of secrets. As if she was reading Zaiba's mind, Layla went over to the built-in wardrobe and opened it up. It was not a wardrobe after all but—

"Another hidden room!" Zaiba breathed. This was incredible. She poked her head inside. There wasn't much in there apart from some dusty old furniture and faded paintings stacked against the far wall.

"Wow, come and look at this, Ade!" Zaiba's voice echoed around the dusty room.

"Naaah, there's nothing in there anyway." Ade wasn't even looking, he was playing on his phone again.

Wait a minute...

"How do *you* know there's nothing in here?" Zaiba swivelled round suddenly. Ade's head shot up, blood rushing to his face.

"Just a guess," he stumbled.

"Have you been to this house recently?" Zaiba was putting the pressure on now. If Ade knew something, she wanted to hear about it.

"No! Anyway, shouldn't you be focusing on investigating or whatever it is you're pretending to do?" He raised an eyebrow at Zaiba.

Zaiba scowled. Fine. He didn't want to talk. Maybe she could find out more from Sefi and Max later.

"Now can I show you one of my favourite places?" Layla sang out, not waiting for an answer before dashing out into the corridor. "It's in the library!"

Zaiba's heart leaped and she raced after Layla, not caring this time if Ade kept up. She was finally going to see a murphy door in real life!

The library was still and dark as Layla scurried in, weaving round the tables and chairs with ease. Zaiba wasn't so familiar with the layout of the impressive room so she spent a few moments trying to locate the light switch, finally finding the gold-plated button high up on the wall. Before she flipped it down however, she took a moment in the gloom to retrieve a couple of the books that had been marked with the warning message. She made sure to choose a book marked with an 'A' as it was written in an interesting way – almost like it was wearing a little hat. When they were safely stored away in her backpack, she flicked on the switch.

Once the room was illuminated Zaiba had a sudden moment of shock. Layla had disappeared!

"Under here!" A little muffled voice came from somewhere inside the room.

Zaiba frowned. "Layla, I'm sorry but we don't have time to play hide-and-seek, we have to investigate this secret passageway."

"She is," a voice said from behind her. Ade had caught up. "I mean, she must be in the secret spot."

A creak from the far corner of the room allowed Zaiba to hone in on where Layla was hidden. There was an antique bureau that was being used as more of a storage table than a place for writing important letters. Beneath the pull-out table were two cabinet doors, and Zaiba noticed that one was slightly ajar.

"I'm not in the secret spot – yet!" Layla poked her head round the cabinet door and grinned at them. "I need your help, Ade. The lever to open the secret door is in here but it's – ugggghhh!" Layla gave it a heave and grunted with the effort. "*It's too stiff.*"

Ade looked very pleased with himself as sauntered over to the bureau, rolling up the sleeves of his shirt with their tortoiseshell buttons and tucking his phone away. Zaiba could tell his parents had made him dress up *extra* fancy for the occasion.

Layla scooted out of the cupboard and Ade's top half disappeared inside. Layla instructed Zaiba to stand with her in front of a particularly tall and thin bookcase, directly next to the bureau. Ade scrabbled about a bit until Zaiba heard the noise of what sounded like a huge clock being wound up. Some very old metal gears were crunching and sliding into place until... *Clunk.*

The bookcase directly in front of Zaiba began slowly opening in on itself, as though it was folding on hinges along its right side.

Zaiba actually squealed with delight. She had *never* seen that before! She couldn't help wishing Ali and Poppy were here with her to witness this moment.

At forty-five degrees the door ground to a halt.

"It used to open all the way but now it's rusty," Layla explained. "My dad used to help me push it open."

Ade quickly got to his feet and came to join them, not wanting to miss out on another chance to prove his strength. As a three they pushed together until the door was completely open.

Small stone steps led upwards from the gap into a dark hallway. There were old iron fixtures on the wall where Zaiba guessed candles used to be lit. For now, they would use her torch to light the way.

"Detective's log," Zaiba gulped in excitement, she could barely get the words out. "Layla has located the murphy door in the library, accessed through a lever hidden in the bureau. We are entering the secret passageway now. Notes and findings to follow."

Zaiba crept forwards in the darkness, guided only by the beam of light from her torch.

"How far does it go?" she whispered to Layla, who was following close behind her.

"Hmmm, Daddy said he thought it went right the way out to the back of the house. But look – it's been boarded up. We never went any further."

Sure enough, as Zaiba squinted into the middle distance she saw that two old boards of wood had been haphazardly stuck up across the passageway.

"Maybe there's a risk of the roof falling in," Ade commented from somewhere behind in the dark. "We had to do that before we had our state-of-the-art skylight put in."

Even in the middle of an investigation, Ade had to fit a brag in somewhere.

As Zaiba checked out the wooden boards her torch picked up a flash of something silver on the floor. Layla saw it too and she bent down to pick it up for Zaiba. She was closer to the ground after all.

"It's an earring." Zaiba was confused. "A very shiny earring." That didn't make sense – the floor was covered in decades of grime. Shouldn't the earring have been covered in dust too?

"Maybe it's one of Courtney's," Layla suggested.

"Come on, let's back out." Making use of her phone's flash, Zaiba took a few snaps before they finally exited the passageway, her eyes adjusting to the bright light. After putting the earring in an evidence bag and marking it with the time and location found, Zaiba turned to the last matter of business for her team.

"Layla, there's one last thing I'd like to check out—"

"Please say it doesn't involve any more running," Ade sighed. "This shirt is way too expensive to be getting sweaty."

"We can walk there," Zaiba reassured him. She didn't want Ade's patience running thin, as she might need him for this next operation. "You know the trapdoor in the corridor that leads from the right side of the foyer?"

Layla's eyebrows furrowed together. "Yes ... but ... I've never been in there. Daddy says it doesn't open."

Olivia had said that too... Zaiba kept a neutral expression.

"Even so, I'd like to have a look if that's OK. Maybe

Ade could find a way to open it," Zaiba said, appealing to his ego.

Sure enough, Ade smiled and seemed more than enthusiastic to lead the way back to the foyer.

"It could just be that you need someone strong enough to prise it open," he explained as he strode ahead of them. "Or there might be a mechanism holding it in place. I'm sure I can work it out."

Zaiba bit her lip to stop from giggling. Ade was trying to help and she was grateful, even if it meant listening to his boasting!

They gathered round the square panel in the corridor and Zaiba reached out, giving a tentative pull on the small hole carved out on one side. The door didn't move.

"I bet there's another hidden switch!" Ade started sliding on the wooden floor pressing in random spots and looking back to the trapdoor to see if it had miraculously opened.

Zaiba knelt down to join him and began pressing her own thumb into cracks and bumps across the ancient floor. They met in the middle and were both so busy inspecting the varnished wooden tiles that they knocked heads.

"Ow!" Ade sat back on his heels, grinning as he rubbed his temple. "Actually, Zaiba, you've given me an idea."

Her breath caught in her throat. "What?"

"What's better than one head?"

She knew the answer immediately. "Two!"

Ade held up his thumb. "And the same might be true for thumbs."

Zaiba *thought* she understood. The two of them scrambled back towards the trapdoor. "We've been looking for one switch," she gasped, "but we need to find two!"

Ade placed his thumb over the hole Zaiba had tried before, ready to press. Zaiba looked and looked around the edge of the trapdoor, but she couldn't see another one. "I don't understand..." she mumbled.

"What's this?" Layla was pointing to a small, round disc cut into the wood panelling on the wall.

Zaiba leaped up. "Well done, Layla!" She went over to the disc and placed the pad of her thumb against it.

A perfect fit. A grown-up could have reached between the two buttons, but not one small detective – it took two of them!

She looked back at Ade – her second detective. "Ready?" If their theory was right, there would be a whole mechanism running beneath the floor and up the wall, to allow the trapdoor to open. How clever!

Ade began to count down. "One, two..."

On the word three, they both pressed their thumbs.

Ping!

The trapdoor clicked open.

Ade looked at Zaiba, open-mouthed. "We did it!"

Zaiba went to his side, as he climbed to his feet.

Below the trapdoor were some narrow wooden steps, leading down into a gloomy darkness. Zaiba couldn't even see how far down it went.

Then she saw it.

A muddy footprint on the wooden staircase.

A *wet* muddy footprint.

Zaiba's suspicions had been correct.

They weren't the first people to open the trapdoor recently. "Someone has been down here."

Zaiba looked up at her companions and saw little Layla clutching her hands together in worry. This was a bit too scary for her.

"Ade, would you cover me? I'm going to investigate further, I don't know how strong these wooden steps are – we might not all be able to go down."

Ade puffed his chest out with pride and actually saluted. He liked being security! He crouched on one knee so he was ready to spring down into the basement if Zaiba needed him.

Zaiba's heart was beating faster and she tried to clear all thoughts of evil jinn or angry ghosts from her mind. She took a deep breath and gently tested her weight on the first step. The old wood creaked but held up OK. She took the next few steps just as carefully, but as the wood seemed in good enough condition she made her way swiftly down the final few steps. It was now pitch-black. Zaiba silently thanked Aunt Fouzia for reminding her to fully charge her torch batteries and she clicked it on yet again.

Down in the basement it was cramped and messy. It was filled with loads of old junk – broken chairs, a very battered tin washing machine and a stack of bricks. Even if Jay, Courtney or Jack had been able to open the trapdoor, they certainly wouldn't have wanted their children poking about down here – it was dangerous. In one of the walls Zaiba spotted a box, set into the brick and locked with a twisty combination code.

Aha, now what could be hiding in there?

But Zaiba had no time to explore.

Above her, the trapdoor *slammed* shut.

"Ade? Layla?" She couldn't help her voice rising higher in pitch. There was no answer. What had happened? Zaiba felt her hands turn cold and clammy. She was underground, in the dark.

All on her own.

9
AN UNDERGROUND INVESTIGATION

Panic rose in Zaiba's chest but she quickly pushed it back down. She could hear muffled sounds from above her. *What was going on?* With the trapdoor shut her torchlight seemed much dimmer and the darkness in the corners of the room loomed large. If a ghost was going to get her, it would *definitely* be now. Her heart started to beat faster – but something she'd read earlier flashed across her mind. Something from her Eden Lockett book.

Scrabbling in the dark she located *The Haunting of Hay Hall* in her backpack and shimmied it out. Luckily, the beam from her torch provided enough light for her to flick through the pages, to chapter nine.

In the margins her ammi had written in bold writing:

In an emergency there are two types of people: The panickers who act before they think and the leaders who think before they act.

Zaiba knew which one she wanted to be. She snapped the book shut, put it back in her bag and took a deep breath. *Think*, first. There were two other people who knew she was down here, she wouldn't be left alone forever. That thought helped Zaiba relax. And now that she wasn't panicking, she could focus on the voices above her. Zaiba recognized Ade and Layla, but there was someone else... Was it Alexandra, the property developer who was friends with Jack? She concentrated hard and was able to pick out a few words – it definitely sounded like her. Ah! So Ade and Layla must have closed the trapdoor to keep Zaiba's investigation hidden. A smart move. She started to feel less scared.

Seeing as she was stuck down here for the time being, Zaiba knew the best thing to do was make the most of it and keep searching. She flashed the light of her torch at the broken furniture pieces and piles of bricks. Hang on.

The bricks piled up by the walls were small, rectangular and reddish. Sort of like the ones that decorated the doorways on the outside of the house. Maybe these were left over from building work?

But there were some other bricks too, strewn about at the foot of the stairs. Ones that still carried chips of the mortar that had stuck them together. A hefty metal chisel lay on its side next to them. *They look as though they've been pulled out of a wall!* Zaiba thought. She picked up a brick, turning it over in her hands. Heavy and orange, it was remarkably similar to the one that had been thrown through the window. She decided to pop it in her backpack to take up to their crime-scene headquarters for comparison. Her backpack sagged under the weight.

She took a few snaps of where the bricks lay and as the flash of the camera lit up the room, it revealed a space underneath the staircase. Zaiba bent down and shuffled underneath the creaky wooden steps. A paint pot – lid open with a paintbrush resting on top – was sitting on some planks of wood. Zaiba reached out and touched the paintbrush.

"Still wet," she whispered, rubbing the red paint between her fingers.

There was another tin next to the paint pot, this one containing some coloured pens labelled, 'multi-surface markers'. Zaiba popped the cap off of one and the smell of the dye was strong enough to overpower the damp in the basement. Zaiba wrinkled her nose. Those fumes couldn't be good for a person. She quickly popped the lid back on. Next to the tin of pens, a scrap of paper had been left on the floor. In one of the thick red markers, someone had written *Leave!*

Zaiba tutted and shook her head. Someone was definitely up to mischief. She felt around in her backpack for an evidence bag and pulled one out to slide the note inside. She picked up the note by the edges so as not to destroy any useful clues.

Suddenly, there was a rumbling of footsteps above her and a flood of yellow light came pouring into the basement. It took Zaiba a few seconds of blinking before Ade and Layla came into focus.

"Zaiba!" Layla called.

"Are you OK?" Ade seemed genuinely concerned – he was taking his new role as security guard very seriously.

Zaiba scrabbled up the wooden steps, brushing dust and debris off her shalwar kameez. Another party outfit dirtied from investigating – Jessica wouldn't be pleased.

As soon as Zaiba was out of the basement, Layla grabbed her and squeezed her hard. "I'm so sorry we shut you in there, you must have been so scared!"

Zaiba hugged her back. "It's OK, you did exactly the right thing. Thank you." She looked at Ade and smiled. She knew it must have been his quick thinking to shut the door when Alexandra appeared. "Did I hear Alexandra up here?"

Ade nodded. "Yep, she asked us what we were doing so we said that Layla had dropped one of her toys down the hole in the floor. She didn't see the trapdoor open so I think she bought it."

Zaiba considered this for a moment. "But what was she doing here?"

"I wondered that too." Ade seemed pleased with himself. "We asked her if she needed help with something but she said she was just looking for the garden to get some fresh air. I guess everyone's been shaken up by the window smashing."

"Good work, Ade. You too, Layla. Plus, I found some new pieces of evidence." She held out her sagging backpack. "Come on, let's take it to HQ!"

Their HQ was empty when Zaiba, Ade and Layla stepped inside. The others were clearly still busy out in the field investigating. That or Ali's chocolate mousse was taking longer than expected to whip up.

Carefully Zaiba pulled the heavy brick out of her backpack and laid it down on the desk. It was certainly a relief not to have to lug it around any more. "Ade, can you get me the brick that was used to smash the window? It's in the top drawer of that cupboard."

With great care, Ade retrieved the brick and placed it down next to their latest find. All three of them stared hard at the two objects, but it was painfully clear. They looked exactly the same!

"Wow," Layla breathed. "What else did you find?"

"This note," Zaiba said grimly, pinning the message up on the board. From her backpack, she slid out one of the books with the letter 'a' painted on it in red.

She compared the letters in the note and on the book's spine. Both were written in the same way, with the extra curve on top.

It was the same handwriting!

"What does this mean?" Layla asked, her eyes darting from the book, to the brick, to the note.

Zaiba turned to both her and Ade with a serious expression. "It means that whoever was down in that basement is responsible for throwing a brick through the Booker's window and leaving them menacing notes. Somebody who wants to scare them."

Ade puffed out his cheeks in wonder. "But why?"

"Well." Zaiba zipped up her backpack and slung it over her shoulders. "That's what I'm hoping Olivia and Poppy's interviews might help us with. It's time we go see what they've found out!"

10
UNCOVERING THE PRINTS

The grand reception room was buzzing with activity and chatter once again as Zaiba wandered among the party guests. The initial shock of the dramatic events had worn off and the surprise had turned into excitement. Courtney was pacing the room with a platter of canapes, eager to keep everyone happy while they waited for dessert. Jack had turned the music up. Zaiba scanned the room, trying to locate Poppy and Olivia to see how far they'd got with collecting information.

A hand caught Zaiba's and she looked back to see her dad smiling at her. He leaned down and whispered in her ear, "How's the investigation going, Agent Zaiba?"

Hassan was intrigued but Zaiba also knew he wanted to check she was safe. A brick thrown through the window was no laughing matter.

"You know I can't reveal details of the case, Dad." Zaiba tapped the side of her nose – something she'd copied from her aunt Fouzia, who always did the same when she was keeping something secret.

Hassan chuckled and stuck his bottom lip out in mock sadness.

"Have you seen Pops?" Zaiba asked and Hassan pointed to the sofas. Zaiba gave her dad a kiss on the cheek and headed off, spotting Poppy's blond hair through the crowd.

She found her and Olivia chatting to Jay, Isabela and Anita, and the talkative Laurence. Poppy was good at interviewing people without letting them know they were being interviewed, which was why Zaiba had given her this task. But even she was finding it hard to get a word in edgeways as Laurence blabbed on.

"And of course the *real* treasure of Beckley town is the nature reserve on the east side of Green Lake. Did you know that it actually began its life as the king's hunting ground back in 1603—"

"I did know that actually," Anita managed to cut in. "I grew up here so we learned it at school."

Laurence looked blankly at her for a second and then forged ahead. "Yes, so in 1603 the king decided to cultivate a wood on the area..."

Zaiba zoned out. At this rate, they'd never learn anything of use. She could see the frustration on Poppy's face – this had obviously been going on a long time. Zaiba tuned back in to hear the end of Laurence's sentence.

"... but now that they've cleared some of that land they ought to build a housing complex there. There's enough space and think of the revenue it would bring to the area!"

Nobody had anything to say to this and Poppy seized the moment. "So, Zaiba, we still don't know what happened with the lights..." she prompted.

Zaiba picked up on her friend's cue. "I know, it's so strange." She watched the expressions on the group's faces for any reactions. "Did anyone notice anything before the lights went out?"

Jay shook his head and Laurence blew air out of his mouth with an exaggerated 'nope' expression.

"I didn't see anything," Isabela said unexpectedly. "I, uh, was looking for the bathroom."

"Yes and I—" Anita cut herself short, suddenly seeming worried. "Never mind."

There was an awkward silence where everyone eyeballed each other.

"Why do you ask?" Laurence cocked his head to one side, looking at Zaiba.

"No reason." Zaiba smiled and quickly tugged Poppy's hand to leave the conversation. Suspicions had been raised. Zaiba heard Olivia behind her politely asking the group, "May I take your empty glasses for you?"

Good work, Liv! Zaiba thought, reminding herself to thank Olivia later. Olivia passed them on the way to the kitchen and winked. She was carrying three glasses on a tray ready for fingerprint inspection by Ali and Flora.

Poppy gestured silently to Jack who was speaking with Ade's dad, Max, and Alexandra.

"What did Jack say Alexandra's job was again?" Poppy whispered as they approached the group.

"A property developer," Zaiba whispered back. "I think it's something to do with buying property and improving it?"

Poppy looked unimpressed and Zaiba couldn't blame her. It wasn't the most interesting topic of conversation.

As they neared the group, Zaiba was relieved to hear they were speaking about something relevant to the investigation.

"Well, it's always difficult wiring these old houses." Jack scratched his head. "It can go wrong sometimes but we wanted to keep all the original light fittings in the house the same."

"Yes, well, keeping the house authentic is the most important thing of all," Max said sternly. "You should always stick to the original design."

Alexandra raised her eyebrows. "I'm not so sure, Max. With respect, I do think we have to keep up with the times. For example, you wouldn't want to keep all that exposed surface wiring, it's so unsightly. It's much better to have them properly insulated, especially if you're keeping your old fuse box."

Goodness, Zaiba thought. *Adults really know how to party. Could they be having a more boring conversation?* Still, she kept listening for any clues.

"That's exactly what we did!" Jack exclaimed. "Although we couldn't locate the old fuse box. We had to install a newer model. Great minds think alike, I suppose."

"Or the sheep follows the herd..." Max grumbled.

Ouch. Another awkward silence. Poppy cleared her throat.

"That's a lovely necklace, Alexandra." Poppy was doing her best to diffuse the tension. "I love the beading – very in this season."

Alexandra touched her necklace lightly and smiled. "Thank you, I made it myself."

Zaiba suddenly felt a presence and turned to see that Olivia had materialized behind them. She was as quiet as a ghost! Zaiba kept that in mind for if they had to do any future silent sleuthing.

"If you'd like a top-up I could get you all a fresh glass?" Olivia offered sweetly, reaching out to take the glasses. She wasn't really waiting for an answer – they needed those fingerprint samples! Zaiba gave her a secret thumbs up. They'd got a system going now and it was working brilliantly.

There was only one group left to infiltrate. Zaiba and Poppy excused themselves and pottered over to the sofa area where Zaiba's parents, Poppy's mum, Courtney and Sefi were talking. It seemed like Hassan was cracking all his best dad jokes because Jessica was laughing heartily while everyone else looked confused. Jessica was the only person Zaiba had met who found Hassan's jokes *hilarious*. Most people only found them funny because they made no sense at all.

"Ah, here comes my little butterfly." Emma reached out and pinched Poppy's cheeks. Poppy instantly turned bright red – now was not the time for babying, she was in the middle of a case!

"And my little worm." Hassan ruffled Zaiba's plaits, chuckling. (Another joke that only Jessica found funny.) Zaiba slapped his hand away with a cheeky smile.

"Zaiba, we were just talking about what a shame it is that all that beautiful stained glass was broken." Jessica's expression darkened. As an art teacher she knew the importance of such skilled craftsmanship – especially as detailed as the stained glass.

"Yes, watch your step. We've swept up most of the glass but there might be some pieces left." Courtney pointed at a dustpan and brush pushed to the side of the room, well away from the guests. It was filled with the shards of glass.

"Have you heard anything from the police about when they might arrive?" Zaiba asked. She still felt there was so much more they could solve!

"They're certainly taking their time..." Courtney sounded frustrated. "They phoned from their car. They've been cut off by a fallen tree!"

Zaiba noticed that Sefi was fixated on picking out the

biggest pieces of glass from the dustpan, sighing as she inspected the damage on each one. "This stained-glass window was over 120 years old." She shook her head. "It was a fundamental part of this house! A historic artefact!"

Jessica bent down next to Sefi and put her hand on her shoulder. "It's a real tragedy," she agreed. "The artistry of the colours and shapes was so special."

Sefi looked up at Jessica and smiled – the first time Zaiba had seen her do so this evening.

"Yes, it truly was," Sefi replied enthusiastically and she straightened up. "Don't you think the addition of the dragonflies was unusual for the period?"

Wow, Sefi had really warmed to Jessica. This was the only time this evening she'd spoken without making a dig. It must be where Ade got his standoffishness from. Zaiba looked over to where Ade was standing with his dad, back to playing on his phone. He looked miserable and Zaiba suddenly felt sorry for him.

"The stained glass was very beautiful. I'm just afraid we won't have enough money to replace it for the time being. Perhaps it will have to be a clear pane for a while," Courtney added to the conversation, sharing her disappointment.

Sefi's smile instantly fell and her face was like thunder. Zaiba felt awful for Courtney. She'd hate to be on the receiving end of that hard look. Just when it seemed like they were on the brink of yet *another* awkward silence, Hassan came to the rescue.

"Yeah, it will be a real *pane* to fix. Get it? Like a window pane." Hassan looked from face to face with a cheesy grin. Poppy and Zaiba actually laughed this time — mainly in relief.

Olivia appeared beside Poppy and Zaiba, smiling. "What's everyone laughing about?"

"Oh, just me being a comedy genius." Hassan winked. Zaiba rolled her eyes.

"Here, everyone, let us replace your empty glasses." All together this time, Zaiba, Poppy and Olivia retrieved the glasses from the adults and scurried off to the kitchen. They'd managed to collect a glass from each guest and a plate from Isabela who wasn't drinking anything. It was fingerprint-matching time!

The girls entered the kitchen triumphantly, holding the last pieces for testing, and burst into giggles. Flora and Ali were covered top to toe in chocolate!

"Have you been using chocolate to uncover the fingerprints this time?" Poppy laughed.

Ali looked sheepish but couldn't help laughing too. "We might have gone a bit overboard with the dark chocolate for the mousse. But don't worry, it hasn't got in the way of the testing."

"Happy to hear it!" Zaiba patted Ali on the head – the only part of his body not covered in sticky chocolate.

"The only thing is," Flora admitted, "we keep getting the glasses mixed up and having to start again."

Olivia put her hands on her hips. "There *are* a lot of glasses... How can we tell them apart?"

Zaiba's eyes flashed with excitement. There was only one thing that could save this situation – stationery! She kept labels in her backpack for the evidence bags, but they could definitely serve more than one purpose.

"Here!" Zaiba got out a roll of the white labels and

started marking them with each guest's name. "Stick these to the work surface and place the matching glass on top of it. We can't stick the label directly to the glass as it might damage the fingerprint."

"I never thought your love of stationery would actually be useful," Ali teased. Zaiba whacked him on the arm, prompting a half-joking push about.

"Focus, you two!" Poppy reminded them.

They set to work, matching each identified fingerprint with its matching label. At one point, Ali and Flora couldn't remember whose glass belonged to who, between Courtney and Anita. But luckily Poppy came to the rescue.

"This glass has a red lipstick mark, the colour Courtney has been wearing this evening. Whereas this glass has a matte deep purple – the edgier look Anita's rocking."

Zaiba was impressed yet again with how observant Poppy was when it came to style!

"And people say that fashion isn't important!" Poppy shook her head in wonder.

After this confusion had been cleared up, they'd finally been able to identify all the fingerprints found on the back door. Ali listed them aloud as Zaiba wrote them down in her notebook:

Fingerprints found on the back door

Booker Family:
Courtney
Flora
Jack
Olivia

Other:
Alexandra
Anita
Jay

Zaiba, Poppy, Olivia, Flora and Ali all peered down together at the list. Olivia was the first to speak. "It makes sense that my family's fingerprints are on there, right? It's our house."

Everyone murmured in agreement.

"But Alexandra?" Poppy asked.

Zaiba thought back to when Alexandra had first arrived at the party. "Alexandra said she had come in through the back door by mistake." Zaiba noted that down next to her name in the book.

"Jay used to live in this house." Ali tapped the paper for Zaiba to write that down. "Fingerprints have been successfully identified on surfaces that were made forty years ago. It's very possible that Jay's would still be there from before the summer." Zaiba scribbled this all down. Ali's talent for memorizing facts was endlessly useful.

"So that leaves just one person." Zaiba looked down at the notebook and stared at the name hard. "What was Anita doing at the back door?"

11
CREEPING IN THE SHADOWS

If there were two things that went well together, it was chocolate mousse and crime solving! *It is very important to keep your energy up during a long investigation*, Zaiba thought as she finished off her pot of gooey chocolate mousse. Once it was all gone, they packed up the fingerprint-evidence papers.

"We'll take these up to headquarters while you two serve dessert," she told Ali and Flora. "Meet us up there when you're done."

"And bring any leftovers!" Poppy added licking her lips. "That raspberry coulis was amazing!"

Zaiba had to practically drag Poppy away from the

trays of chocolate mousse to follow her upstairs. If Ali was the biggest fan of cooking, then Poppy was the biggest fan of eating! Poppy was always willing to test Ali's new recipes and offer feedback.

But there was no time for feedback now, there was a crime to solve. And precious time was ticking away – the police chief could have cleared the tree out of the road and be on his way as they spoke.

Back in their crime-scene headquarters, Zaiba carefully organized the new evidence into some empty drawers. In no time at all Ali and Flora were racing through the door, and they'd managed to ditch their messy aprons.

"Everyone wanted dessert, so it was easy!" Ali explained, catching his breath. "Now bring us up to speed."

That was music to Zaiba's ears. The teams had been broken up but they needed to bring together all their knowledge to get the full picture.

"I found these in the basement." She placed the brick and the note on a table before the gathered team of detectives. "First, the note."

Olivia and Flora gasped.

"*Leave!* How horrible…" Olivia grimaced. "And written in that same blood-red colour as the message on the books."

"Look closely," Zaiba said, moving on quickly before they got too upset. "The handwriting also matches that found on the books in the library."

"What books?" Ali and Flora asked.

Zaiba showed him the books she had taken from the library. Ali examined them and then held the note up to his nose. "Ah, I see it now. Well spotted!"

"Thank you." Zaiba couldn't help a flush of pride. Aunt Fouzia would be so proud of her. "And this brick – that I found in the basement – matches the one thrown through the window."

"Any leads on who it could be?" Ali asked.

Poppy pointed to the map they'd made earlier of the reception room and jabbed a finger at Anita. "Both Isabela and Anita have been acting *very* weirdly if you ask me. They're vague when you ask them a question *and* Isabela wasn't there when the lights went off, remember?"

The group silently nodded, taking in this information.

"But then there's that argument between Max and Alexandra about us renovating the house," Olivia added. "What was all that about? Max seemed really angry."

Zaiba tapped her foot quickly against the floor, chewing her lip. All of those people were acting suspiciously. She also couldn't rule out the fact that both Jay and Laurence know their way around the house very well – including knowledge of the back entrance. There were so many ideas floating around in Zaiba's head, it was hard to pin one down to focus on.

"And none of this explains why someone would have stolen Courtney's bracelet earlier or thrown a brick through the window!" she blurted out.

Olivia opened her mouth to say something but then shook her head and clammed up.

"No, go on, Liv," Zaiba encouraged her. "There are no silly suggestions!"

Olivia paused before whispering, "What about our

original theory? *Could* it be ghosts? Mischievous jinn or angry soldiers?"

Flora didn't scoff this time. From her pale complexion and strained eyes, everyone could see Olivia was very worried.

"It's a fair point," Zaiba pondered, "but I think we can rule out the supernatural."

Ali was smiling from ear to ear. "I knew it couldn't be ghosts. It just isn't scientifically proven."

Zaiba gazed up at the large corkboard above her, with the scraps of evidence, notes, drawings and floorplans all overlapping on the space. This needed order – just like her busy mind. Then inspiration struck her.

"Poppy, do you remember when we watched that one television special they made of Eden Lockett's short-story collection?" Zaiba's eyes shone with her idea.

"The one we both agreed to never mention again because it clearly showed Eden doing all the work and the policemen getting ALL the credit?" Poppy replied, sounding angry.

"Yes, that one!" They'd both vowed to deny its

existence for ever after. "Despite it being AWFUL do you remember they did this?" Zaiba opened Courtney's immaculately organized stationery drawer and located some drawing pins and red string. With a pair of scissors, she began snipping bits of string off and using the pins to link pieces of evidence together.

"Everyone shout questions at me!" she instructed. "We'll think out loud."

Zaiba worked quickly, tacking up more pieces of paper with words and names she'd scribbled on to connect with other pieces of paper.

"OK, Laurence knows a lot about the house, because he sold it," Poppy kicked off the proceedings. "But how come Alexandra knows things too? Like that specific detail about the electrics? It's not something people are interested in for fun."

"I'm interested in electrics for fun!" Ali protested, but Zaiba ignored him.

Zaiba quickly linked a piece of red string between

Alexandra in the reception-room map to the floorplan she'd drawn of Oakwood Manor – specifically to the trapdoor. Why did she need to pass by there?

"Why are Max and Sefi so rude to my mum and dad?" Flora called out. "They're always criticizing what we've done to the house!"

"And Sefi seemed to know a lot about the stained glass. How would she know that?" Olivia added.

Zaiba nodded eagerly. She was in full detective mode now, her brain going a mile a minute and her hands just trying to keep up. She put a piece of string between Sefi and Max to Courtney and Jack.

"WHERE WAS ISABELA WHEN THE LIGHTS WENT OFF?" Ali suddenly bellowed, making everyone fall silent. "Sorry, I got excited."

"No worries." Zaiba stood back from the board and examined her handiwork. "I get excited too."

Ali blushed and Zaiba saw that he was trying to sneak a look at Flora to see if she'd noticed his outburst. She had and was clearly trying to cover up a grin with her hand.

"So far we have a lot of suspects and a lot of questions."

Zaiba sighed. "But not a lot of answers."

Zaiba might have let her frustration get the better of her had they not heard a noise that chilled her to the bone.

A loud thud, following by a blood-curdling *scream!*

It was small and high-pitched, and Zaiba knew there was only one girl who could have made that sound.

"Hold on, Layla! We're coming!"

Zaiba spotted her dad in the foyer as they raced down the stairs.

"Where is she?" she called, desperately searching the area for any sign of Layla.

"She's in the conservatory!" Hassan said. "Her dad's with her."

Zaiba rushed down the remaining stairs, with her fellow detectives in hot pursuit. Without realizing it, she had crossed her fingers, hoping that Layla wasn't hurt.

In the conservatory, the patio doors were open and a crowd was huddled round the bottom of the winding iron stairs that led to the balcony. Zaiba spotted Layla in Jay's arms, sitting on the floor. She was upright and seemed OK, but she was holding on to her right ankle.

"Layla! What happened?" Zaiba knelt down next to her and gave her a big hug.

"I was climbing up the stairs because I thought I spotted something at the top, but one of the steps came loose under my feet and I fell." Layla's cheeks were still wet from her tears but she gave Zaiba a brave smile. "I'm OK, I promise."

"I do think you've twisted your ankle though, sweetie." Deep worry lines were etched into Jay's forehead as he examined her tiny ankle. "You shouldn't go walking around outside in the dark!"

"I'm so sorry, Jay. I can't believe this happened!" Courtney's eyes were pleading. "We used those stairs earlier today and they were fine. I don't know what could have happened."

Jack was inspecting the steps, pushing down on the iron railings and testing their strength.

"Maybe they got wet with the rain earlier and she

slipped?" Jessica offered.

"That's the problem with these old houses." Alexandra had been standing in the shadows and Zaiba hadn't realized she was there until she spoke. "They can be dangerous if not maintained properly."

"Are you saying we haven't looked after our house?" Jack was offended.

"Now, now, old chap, I'm sure this wouldn't have happened if she was properly supervised." Laurence cast a look at Jay.

"Excuse me!" Jay bellowed.

"These stairs are original from the time period, they should be purely ornamental!" Max just seemed furious that the stairs were damaged, he hadn't even glanced at poor Layla.

"I hope they aren't damaged beyond repair." Sefi glared at Jack and Courtney.

Zaiba held her breath. This was getting out of hand. Everyone was turning on each other!

As the adults continued arguing over who was to blame, Layla tilted her head up and whispered into

Zaiba's ear. "I think there's a clue at the top of the stairs," she said. "You have to go and find out. You can get on to the balcony through the big bedroom upstairs. Hurry!"

Zaiba squeezed Layla's hand and silently got up, gesturing to Poppy and Olivia to follow her. She didn't want the whole team to come, or it would arouse suspicion from the adults. As she passed Ade in the huddled crowd however, he grabbed her hand and gave her a serious look.

"Be careful, Zaiba," he whispered. Zaiba gave him a firm nod back. She'd let Ade be part of the team and he was truly acting like it. Giving someone a chance paid off!

As they got back into the conservatory and out of earshot, Zaiba asked Olivia to lead them to the master bedroom. She felt a bit rude going into Courtney and Jack's bedroom but this was important! There was too much at stake. Besides, Olivia was with them and it was *her* mum and dad's room... This reasoning made Zaiba feel a bit better about the situation.

Olivia showed them the way to the master bedroom up ahead and Poppy kept watch a few paces back to check they weren't being followed. When Poppy had given them a nod, Olivia eased open the door and they all went in together, shutting it behind them. Olivia switched on a bedside lamp and Poppy sighed in admiration. The room was very beautiful, with a big four-poster bed, a deep red velvet loveseat and matching plush carpet.

"Oh my gosh," Poppy breathed. "Look at that vanity mirror!" She pointed to Courtney's pretty dressing table, holding the most beauty products Zaiba had ever seen! If Poppy started to have a look through them, they'd be here all evening.

"Come on, Pops, there's no time for this. We need to climb out there." Zaiba had spotted the two full-length shuttered windows that opened out on to the balcony. She reached up to pull down the bolts that kept the windows locked, trying to be as gentle as possible so they didn't make a loud scraping noise. Everyone was still downstairs on the patio and now that the arguing had died down, Zaiba, Olivia and Poppy could easily be heard walking around on the balcony. They would have to be silent and stealthy.

Luckily Zaiba knew this was Olivia's strong point!

She held a finger to her lips and motioned Olivia to go first.

Carefully, Olivia tiptoed out on to the balcony and across towards the iron staircase. Once Zaiba was certain their footsteps wouldn't draw attention, she and Poppy followed after. The night was pitch-black outside and a chilly wind made Zaiba's plaits flap in the breeze. She thought that if anyone did see their figures up here in the dark, they'd definitely have a fright!

Silent as mice, they crept along the stone floor of the balcony, avoiding a few large puddles and keeping an eye out for the clue Layla had spotted. Voices floated up from below them and Zaiba recognized one as her dad's, followed by the tinkling of Jessica's laughter. Clearly Hassan was trying out a few more of his jokes to ease the tension.

From up on the balcony the surrounding woods seemed even darker and denser, and Zaiba was surprised just how far they spread outwards. The house was quite isolated from the rest of the town.

Olivia came to a halt ahead of them and started waving frantically at the edge of the balcony, just beyond the top of the stairs. There was something tied to the railings, but if they walked over there, anyone could look up at any moment and spot them. Zaiba knew what she had to do.

Rolling up the bottom of her shalwar to the thigh, she dropped to her hands and knees on the damp balcony floor and edged forwards. She was worried about the mess she'd make but collecting this piece of evidence was way more important than getting muddy knees!

As slowly and carefully as possible, she reached to untie the object from the balcony railing before backing up the way she came. When she had made it to the hidden part of the balcony, she stood and saw that Poppy was looking at her clothes in dismay. They were pretty mucky but she'd secured the item. They headed back inside to the master bedroom to identify it.

"Brrrrrrr, it was freezing out there!" Poppy shivered as Olivia secured the doors shut again.

"I'm going to need a wash." Zaiba looked down at

her hands and legs, which were covered in wet dirt. "But we've got this!"

She held up the evidence to the light and all three of them recognized it.

"Laurence's scarf!" Poppy gasped. It was blue striped and now, slightly damp, the tassels hung limply in the breeze.

"What was Laurence doing out on the balcony?" Olivia asked. "And why did he leave his scarf there?"

Zaiba was just as perplexed as they were. "I'm not sure. But Layla is turning out to have a real agent's instinct." She popped the scarf into her backpack. "We need to search the patio but first we'll have to get everyone to come inside. We can't have them asking questions. Come on."

"Uh, Zaiba." Poppy looked her up and down. "Maybe you should clean up in the bathroom first."

"Yeah, we wouldn't want Mum and Dad to know we've been out on the balcony," Olivia agreed.

Zaiba was reluctant to delay the investigation but she knew that Poppy and Olivia were right. They headed to the main bathroom before they went back to the reception room. As they were about to turn on to the corridor, Zaiba heard voices and she raised her hand quickly to halt Poppy and Olivia.

Peering round the corner, she spotted Isabela emerging from the main bathroom, dabbing her eyes and pale as a sheet. Anita had been waiting outside and now she slipped an arm through Isabela's, gently leading her back downstairs. As much as Zaiba strained to hear, she couldn't make out their hushed conversation, and eventually the two women disappeared out of sight.

Zaiba quickly told her friends what she'd just seen.

"But there are two bathrooms downstairs," Olivia said, "so there's no need for Isabela to be up here."

"No," Poppy agreed. "Unless..."

Zaiba narrowed her eyes. "Unless she's trying to hide something!"

12
A MOST SUSPICIOUS FIND

How do you convince ten adults to come inside and stay put in one room? Offer them tea and biscuits of course! Hassan had brought some of his homemade ginger snap biscuits as a party gift – no one could resist those. Ali had got his baking talent from their dad!

Zaiba laid them out on the table in the reception room, along with two piping-hot pots of tea, a cafetière of coffee and a jug of milk. Olivia even got out the fancy cups and saucers her mum saved for special occasions. This was, after all, a *very* special occasion.

"Excuse me, everyone," Zaiba announced at the patio doors. "Tea and biscuits are ready in the reception room if you'd like to come through."

There was a general noise of appreciation and, like magic, the adults filed in one by one through the conservatory and into the reception room, where Ali and Flora were resuming their roles as mini-waiters. Zaiba couldn't understand why grown-ups seemed to *love* hot drinks so much.

Once everyone had left the patio, she followed them into the reception room to ensure there were no stragglers.

Ali was pouring tea carefully into Courtney's teacup. "Can I offer you some milk, madame?" he said in his best French accent. Courtney giggled, charmed by his waiter routine. Zaiba was pleased to see Courtney enjoying herself again.

Meanwhile Flora was on hand offering up biscuits to Laurence and Alexandra who were back in conversation about housing (*snooze!*). They took two biscuits each – the ginger snap biscuits were always a hit.

Over by the sofas, Zaiba heard Olivia ask Isabela if she'd like a tea or coffee but she shook her head. "Perhaps some hot water and lemon?"

"I'm not sure we have lemons, but I'll check."

Anita seemed worried. "It's quite late anyway. Shall we go home now, darling?"

"No, I'm fine," Isabela snapped. When she realized that Olivia was looking at her oddly she added, "Um, Courtney said we can't leave until the police arrive anyway."

Olivia backed out of the prickly situation quickly, making an excuse about finding a lemon, and took her place next to Zaiba. "That was awkward," she whispered.

Now that the guests had settled back into the reception room and were occupied with their drinks and biscuits, it was time to check out the patio. Zaiba texted the Snow Leopard Detective Agency UK group chat, which she had temporarily added Ade to for the evening.

Agents! Time to move out and assemble. Meet in conservatory ASAP.

After a few minutes, Zaiba was joined in the conservatory by Poppy, Ali, Ade, Olivia and Flora. Ade must have had to make some excuse to his parents as he was the last to arrive. It was time for a mission briefing. A small hand crept into Zaiba's and she realized Layla had followed them out there. She was very observant!

"Layla, don't you need to rest your ankle?" Zaiba was concerned; she didn't want Layla to hurt herself even more.

"Noooo, it's all better. Besides, I want to know what you found!" Layla's eyes shone up at Zaiba. Zaiba knew she wouldn't win this argument, so she slid off her backpack and pulled out the end of the scarf to show to the group.

"It's Laurence's scarf, which we found tied to the balcony railings," she explained.

"So, Laurence was up on the balcony?" Ali asked, eyeing the scarf intently. "It's not really the best weather for it."

Zaiba stuffed the scarf back inside her bag and shook her head. She'd been working on another theory, and it was time to share it with the group. "I don't think so. If Laurence had been sneaking around up there, he wouldn't deliberately leave something that could tie him to the scene of the crime. I think the scarf was put there as a trap. The culprit left it there to lure someone up the stairs after meddling with one of the steps. They wanted to hurt someone."

The group fell silent, deep in thought. The messages left with hurtful words were unkind, but wanting to harm someone? That was cruel and dangerous.

Zaiba went outside to the patio area, still damp from the day's downpour, and turned on her torch. There was a small safety light out here, but it wasn't enough to see anything in any real detail. They'd have to look closer.

"Everyone split up and search for clues!"

The flagstones of the patio looked relatively normal, as did the garden furniture. There was a flower bed that lined the perimeter of the patio and Zaiba stepped in further to examine the earth. Any signs of disturbance would be easier to spot in loose dirt. She traced the flower bed all round the sides of the patio, until she came close to the spot where the iron staircase started. Then she saw it. A footprint! Could it match the one they had found out near the pond? For comparison, she took a few photos and zoomed in.

"Hold on, what's that?" she muttered to herself, zooming in further on something shining in the image. She looked once more in the dirt, bending right down until her face was level with some tulips.

"Four screws!" she called, bringing the others rushing over. "And I bet we'll find where they came from on the staircase."

She dropped the screws into Poppy's hands and she gently started up the stairs.

"Layla, how far up were you when you fell?" she called over her shoulder.

"Ummm, about five steps up," Layla called back. "Be careful!"

Zaiba trod as lightly as she could up to the fourth step, and then leaned forwards to inspect the fifth. On the underside she noticed four little holes, all missing their matching screw!

"Just as I thought," Zaiba whispered and she hurried back down the stairs. "Somebody loosened those screws on the steps and then hid the evidence when everyone was out here fussing over Layla."

"But that's so mean!" Olivia was outraged. Zaiba, Poppy and Ali were used to the actions of criminals now, but Olivia was still new to all this.

"This proves without a shadow of a doubt..."

The others waited for her to finish her sentence. It was fun to be a detective!

"... that the culprit is currently sitting in the other room! Enjoying tea and biscuits."

As one, the team headed back in from the cold. Olivia pulled Zaiba to one side. "Zaiba, I have to ask. Do you have any idea who is responsible for all this?" She looked tired and anxious.

"I'm about ninety-nine per cent sure I know who it is, Liv. But I just need one more piece of evidence before I make any accusations."

"OK." Olivia yawned and Zaiba gave her a big hug.

"Don't worry, this will all be sorted tonight. I promise."

13
BEAT IT!

"Ah, there you are!" Courtney said as she saw them come in. "Good news, the police chief said he should be here in half an hour. The tree has been shifted! In the meantime, Jack is telling us all about the history of the house." Courtney gestured to Jack to carry on with his story.

The children settled down on the carpet in front of the armchair where Jack was sitting, but Zaiba remained standing.

"So yes, the house was really a marvellous feat of architecture and design. As well as the structure of the frame, which was very ground-breaking for its time, the hidden passageways and rooms make it unique."

"I must say, Jack, I'm impressed with the amount of research you've done into the building," Sefi smiled, in a surprised sort of way.

"It's very important to us that we honour the history of the house and the wishes of Bernard and Madeline Hargreaves."

"Here, here!" Max raised his teacup and everyone did the same in return.

Everyone, that is, except Anita and Isabela, who were slipping out the back of the room into the corridor.

As swiftly and silently as possible, Zaiba snuck along the side of the room and followed the couple.

They were halfway to the foyer when Zaiba managed to catch them up. She reached up on tiptoe and tapped Anita on the shoulder.

"Oh!" She whirled round, looking startled to see Zaiba standing there, as did Isabela who was clutching her stomach.

"It's OK," Zaiba said quietly. "I know why you've been sneaking around."

The women went silent and stared at Zaiba.

Zaiba looked at Isabela. "I hope I'm not being rude but ... you're pregnant, aren't you?"

Isabela's mouth fell open and Anita laughed unexpectedly.

"How did you know?" Isabela asked, her cheeks flushing red.

"My cousin Sam is pregnant too. You've been acting the same as her. Avoiding caffeine, drinking hot water and lemon. And ... er ... being a bit snappy – no offence."

This made Anita chuckle even more and Zaiba noticed the corners of Isabela's mouth twitch upwards.

"I'm sorry for following you out here, but I've been investigating the events of this evening, and I just wanted to clear everything up."

"You're a very clever girl." Isabela smiled. "But you can't tell anyone yet! We're excited but it's too early to share the news. We haven't even told our parents."

Zaiba mimed zipping her mouth shut.

"And I'm sorry I was a bit strange when your friend asked me questions earlier," Anita added. "The truth is, I'd gone to check on Isabela when the lights went out.

I saw someone outside the door through the glass and thought it was her. But then I heard Sefi yell and came back."

So that's why Anita's fingerprints were on the inside of the back door! Zaiba thought, relieved to have cleared up that mystery.

"I've been having bad nausea, running in and out of the bathroom," Isabela explained. Even as she spoke, her face seemed to turn an odd shade of green and she clutched her stomach. Zaiba once again thought that being pregnant sounded miserable.

Isabela and Anita walked quickly to the bathroom as Zaiba made her way back into the reception room, where Jack was keeping his guests hanging on his every word.

"... and before Jay and Layla lived here, the house was briefly owned by a woman who ran the local women's football team! She would organize post-match celebrations in the gardens."

Sefi clapped her hands together in delight. "Oh, that's amazing. *Even I* didn't know that!"

Zaiba couldn't help smiling at her enthusiasm.

Jack was looking puzzled. "But why would you know?" he asked.

Zaiba approved – this was a very good question.

Sefi clearly suddenly realized her mistake and she went beetroot-red. She exchanged a look with Max and he gave her a 'go ahead' gesture with one hand. Ade seemed embarrassed at his mum's outburst and wouldn't look up from the floor.

"Well, actually –" Sefi cleared her throat – "I'm a descendant of Madeline Hargreaves."

"*What?*" Courtney yelped. All evening, Sefi and Max had been rude to them and this was the reason why? Zaiba couldn't get her head around it.

"Why didn't you just tell us rather than being so critical?" Jack shook his head in disbelief.

Sefi took a deep breath and straightened her shoulders. "I suppose I just feel such a family connection to the house and the thought of someone else living here can be *difficult.*"

"But if you feel such a link to the house, then why didn't come round when we first moved in. You never welcomed us to the neighbourhood." Courtney seemed very upset and she wanted answers, which Zaiba could understand.

Sefi blushed and avoided Courtney's gaze. "Just before Jay and Layla moved in, a young couple lived here. Believe it or not, they banned me, Max and Ade from visiting the house any more after I showed just a little bit too much interest in what they planned to do with it."

Zaiba sighed. She *could* believe it.

"We only wanted to know whether they planned to treat the house with the respect it deserves!" Max added emphatically. "But then we did agree that maybe the telephone calls and unplanned visits were a step too far."

Courtney was wringing her hands. "So, have you been behind all the strange things that've been happening recently?"

Sefi clutched her hand to her chest. "Oh gosh, no! I would never do anything to damage the house. And after I heard how invested you are in its history – and how favourably you spoke of my ancestor Madeline – I know you'll be wonderful owners. I'm truly sorry for being so rude."

After a pause, she elbowed Max and he quickly muttered, "My apologies too."

Zaiba raised her eyebrows at Ade who had sneaked a glance up and he shrugged apologetically. But Zaiba couldn't blame him for keeping his parent's secret. It must have been hard for him.

Courtney grabbed Jack's hand and squeezed. She seemed ready to forgive them.

"Sefi, I've put together a scrapbook of Oakwood's history if you'd like to have a look?" Jack offered. "It has some fabulous photos. It's in the kitchen."

Sefi's whole face lit up and she took up Jack's offer at once, following him out into the foyer. Zaiba felt a warm glow in her stomach. Even though this wasn't over yet, she was pleased that Courtney and Jack had made peace with their neighbours.

But the feeling soon gave way when she heard Jack's voice exclaim, "What on earth!"

As quick as a flash, Zaiba sped out into the foyer and down the little stairs to the kitchen.

Sefi and Jack were frozen in shock, staring at the wall above the cooker.

There, in that same red paint, were the words:

BEAT IT!

14
THE SECRET DOOR

Zaiba's mind whirred. Three messages, all written in red paint and in the same handwriting.

STAY AWAY
LEAVE!
BEAT IT!

They were getting angrier as they went on. Zaiba knew for sure that these notes all wanted the same thing – for the Booker family to move out.

Courtney rushed into the kitchen behind Zaiba and burst into tears when she saw the message. "That's it!

I just can't take this any more. We want to do everything we can to restore this house and welcome our neighbours but clearly we aren't wanted here. If someone wants us gone then we should just GO."

She put her head in her hands and Sefi came over to comfort her.

"No, no, Courtney, don't say that." Sefi patted her back.

"Mummy, no, we don't want to leave!" Flora came skittering down the narrow stairs, closely followed by Olivia, Poppy and Ali.

"Yes, we really love it here – especially with our new friends. We'd love the house even if it *was* haunted," Olivia assured her, clinging on to her mum's waist tightly.

"*It's not haunted,*" Flora and Ali chanted.

Zaiba ignored the dramatics and went over to inspect the message. She rubbed the paint between her fingers... *Yep*, it was exactly the same colour as in the tin she'd found in the basement. *And* she'd seen it somewhere else – on a certain guest's scarf earlier that evening.

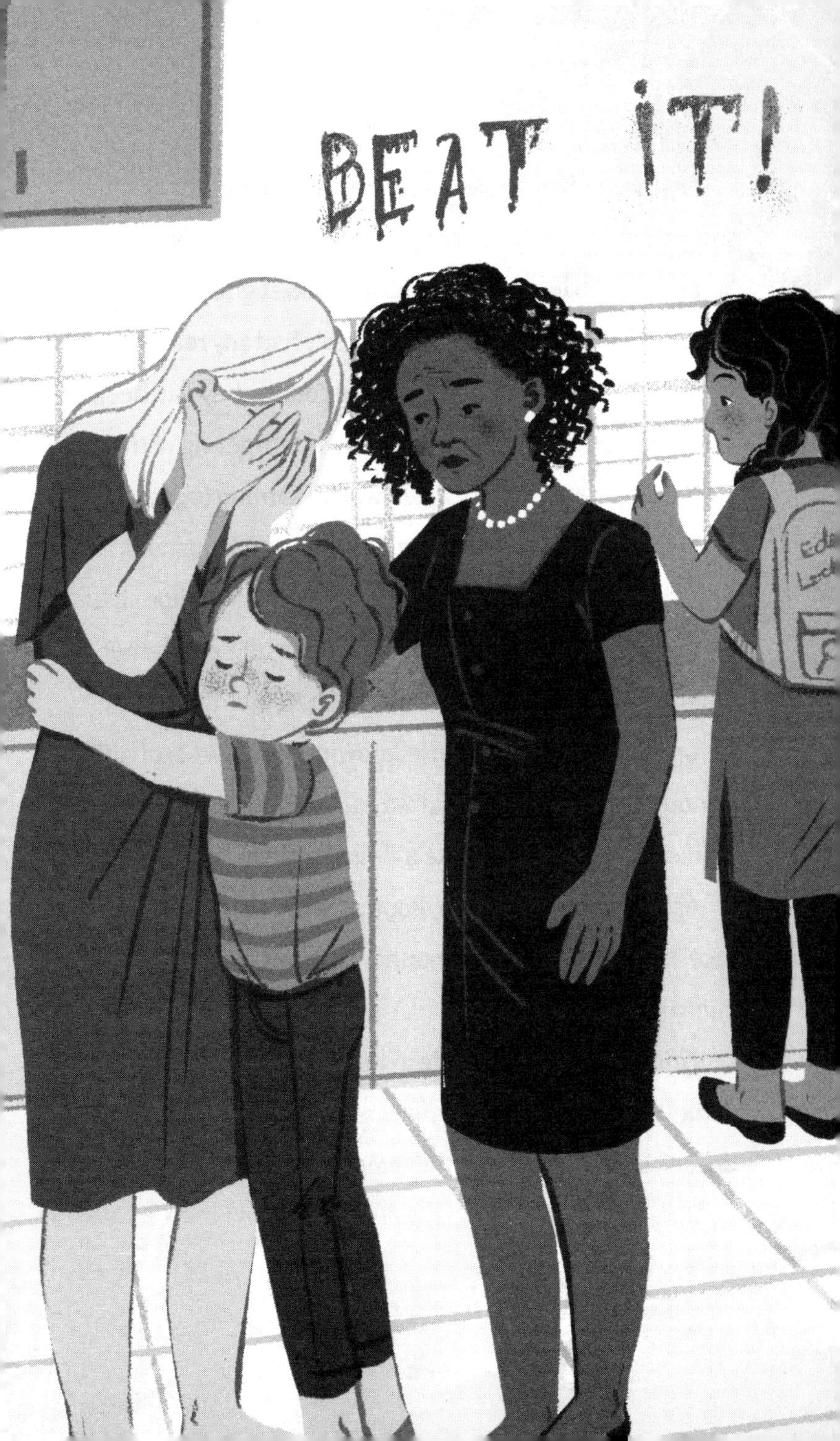
BEAT IT!

On the kitchen floor there were scuffed muddy footprints where someone had left in a hurry. Only someone who had been outside in the wet grass and dirt would have muddy shoes, and nobody had any reason to be out there this evening – unless of course they had been hurling bricks through the windows or tampering with some screws on the staircase. It was all coming together.

Jack and Sefi were leading Courtney back upstairs now that she'd regained her composure. The police chief would soon be here and they wanted to all be together when he arrived. But Zaiba had to share her thoughts before he got there, because knowing him he'd probably announce that the criminal was a neighbour's pet chihuahua and try to make a doggy arrest!

As they left the kitchen, Poppy looked hard at Zaiba's face. "Something's on your mind, I can tell. You're chewing your lip!"

Zaiba decided to confide in her best friend. "There's something about the fingerprints on the door that doesn't seem right. Can I think aloud to you?"

"Fire away."

"Well, we think we have explanations for why everyone's fingerprints are on the back door, but someone's on there *has* to be the culprit. I know it's not Anita. She's been acting weird because Isabela is pregnant."

"Oh, cute!" Poppy squealed.

"I know, but we need to keep it a secret. Alexandra and Laurence… They both came in through the back door so why weren't Laurence's fingerprints on there?" Zaiba was testing Poppy now, she had worked out the answer to this bit.

"The designer gloves!" Poppy clicked her fingers. "Alexandra and Laurence were both wearing gloves when they came in."

"That's right. So Alexandra must have left her fingerprints on the door when she used it *later on*. After she'd taken the gloves off. Probably when she needed to go outside and *throw the brick!*"

They'd reached the reception room now and Zaiba was on a roll. She strode over to the armchair where Alexandra had been sitting when Jack was telling his story and pointed at the floor.

"A muddy footprint!" Poppy whispered.

"Zaiba." Ali tapped her on the shoulder. "Layla just came up to me asking how we knew about a 'secret door'? Do you know what she means?"

Zaiba spun round so fast she startled Ali. "Where is she?"

Ali pointed to the corridor that led from the far side of the reception room to the back door.

All three of them rushed out into the corridor. Layla was standing halfway inside a wooden panel that had opened in the wall. Another hidden passageway!

"Layla, was this door open when you came out here?" Zaiba asked, keeping her voice low.

"Yes!" Layla smiled, but then her expression darkened. "Wait, it wasn't you?"

Zaiba, Poppy and Ali shook their heads.

"Where does this passageway lead?"

Layla beckoned Zaiba in. There was only enough room for one person (or one small person and one very tiny person like Layla). The passageway was narrow and filled with cobwebs, so it was a good thing Ali couldn't fit in as well. Directly in front of her, Zaiba noticed a black box mounted to the wall, almost falling apart, with lots of switches on it.

"The old fuse box is in here!" Zaiba called out to Poppy and Ali. "This must be how the culprit flicked the switch to turn all the lights out." Zaiba wanted to follow this narrow corridor further down into the house but she didn't have time.

"Where does this lead to, Layla?"

"The kitchen!"

Zaiba started to shuffle her way back out of the cramped space. "I wonder if it was a passageway for the servants, so they could easily serve guests in the reception room without having to run up and down the stairs."

"That would have been useful to know when me and Flora were refilling all those drinks," Ali grumbled.

Poppy, once again, looked dismayed at the state of Zaiba's outfit after scrabbling about in the dust. Zaiba let herself be brushed down as she explained her theory.

"The culprit was using this passageway all evening to sneak about. Tripping the lights and sneaking off to the kitchen to write that horrible message when Jack told his story about the history of the house. Plus that passageway in the library – I'm willing to bet it leads out to the locked tunnel by the pond we saw earlier. The culprit must have had a key to that shiny new padlock! Which meant they could access the house whenever they wanted."

Ali looked at Zaiba quizzically. "You keep saying the culprit, but I think you know who it is."

Zaiba rubbed her hands together and focused. "I do."

Layla and Ali gasped, keeping their eyes fixed on their head detective. Poppy gave Zaiba a nod, encouraging her to share her thoughts with the others.

"So, how are we going to expose them?" Poppy asked.

Zaiba hesitated for a moment, but she knew she had the perfect plan – she just had to believe in herself.

"The culprit wanted the Bookers to think that the manor was haunted. Well, let's give them a ghost."

15
A GHOST REVEALED

Zaiba drew herself up tall and prepared to walk back into the reception room. She was going to expose the culprit and put an end to this 'haunting' once and for all. She'd sent Ali to the crime-scene headquarters to collect the evidence for the presentation, while Olivia and Flora were instructed to seal all the secret passageways but the one in the corridor. Even Ade had messaged the group, asking to be security again.

Poppy and Zaiba were in charge of the last bit of preparation. They needed to call Aunt Fouzia.

Zaiba flicked through her contacts and found Aunt Fouzia's number.

"Hello, sweetie. What's the latest?" Aunt Fouzia was always alert.

"We need you over at Oakwood Manor. I'm about to confront the culprit and it would be great to have some backup."

"Say no more, I'm there." Zaiba heard Aunt Fouzia snap the TV off in the background.

"I'll send the address straight away."

"See you in T minus fifteen minutes." Aunt Fouzia clicked off the phone. She didn't waste time saying goodbyes when her niece needed her!

Just then, Ade poked his head round the corner of the doorframe from the reception room. "Uh, you two might want to come in here quickly. We have another guest."

Poppy gave Zaiba a worried look and together they followed him back through to find the police chief hovering next to Courtney and Jack.

"I recognize you." The portly man pointed at Zaiba. "You were at the summer fete when that lady got poisoned."

"The head teacher," Zaiba corrected him. "And I

solved the crime, remember?"

The police chief grinned. "So you did! Maybe you can help me with my enquiries. A break-in, was it?"

Wrong again. Zaiba did her best to hide her frustration with the police chief – she wasn't a rude person, but she couldn't trust him to close the case now that she'd identified the person responsible.

Ali pottered into the room, arms full of pieces of evidence. When he caught sight of the police chief he stopped still, making frantic eyes at Zaiba.

"Actually, Chief, if you wouldn't mind, I'd like to share a quick story first." Zaiba stepped forwards into the middle of the circle of sofas, where the rest of the guests were sitting. This was Ali's cue to start laying out the evidence on the large banquet table at the back of the room.

"I'm looking forward to this," the chief said, rubbing his hands together. After all, he'd seen Zaiba's crime-fighting skills before.

"Zaiba's been helping us all day," Courtney said.

The police chief sat down in an armchair. "I'm all ears!"

Zaiba slid the backpack off her shoulders and placed it on the table. She didn't need her tools any more; it was time to reveal her findings. Olivia and Flora had come back into the room and gave her a big thumbs up, meaning all passageways were secure. Ade had positioned himself by the main entrance to the room and gave Zaiba an OK sign. It was time.

"This is a ghost story so, Poppy, if you wouldn't mind dimming the lights."

Poppy turned off the main lights, leaving just the glow of the yellow lamp in the corner of the room. Courtney had lit candles on the main tables earlier and now their flickering gave an eerie glow to the faces of Zaiba's audience. She noticed that Sefi had grabbed Max's hand when she heard the word 'ghost'. Zaiba cleared her throat and began.

"This is a story about a kind and friendly family. One summer, they decide to move to a beautiful old manor house in the middle of an ancient wood. They are excited to start their new lives and make new friends. But it seems the house has different ideas. One morning shortly after they move in, a vase slides off the hall table smashing into pieces as it falls. The family are shocked. What could have caused the vase to fall all on its own? They try to forget the incident, but things only start to get worse.

"Plates begin flying off shelves in the kitchen while no one's around, toppling to the floor. Furniture changes position seemingly on its own. Jewellery goes missing. The family can't explain the strange happenings any more. There must be a ghost in the house and it *does not like them*.

"Three horrible messages are found – the first written out on book spines, saying *stay away*, the second *leave!* and the third written on the kitchen wall, *BEAT IT!*."

Ali held up the pieces of evidence for the guests to see, making sure the police chief in particular had a good look.

"All the messages are written in blood-red paint. A paint that would later be discovered down in the basement of the old manor. A brick is thrown through the historic stained glass – shattering it into a thousand pieces."

Sefi gave a little sob, still devastated about the destruction. But Zaiba barely noticed, adrenaline was racing through her now and she was on a roll. This was the moment every agent lived for.

"This ghost is aggressive. Smashing a window wasn't enough, so it sneaked around the house using secret passageways, even tampering with the screws on the wrought-iron stairway to cause a small girl to fall and injure herself."

Layla hobbled over to the police chief, majorly exaggerating her injury, but pointing at her ankle defiantly.

Zaiba ploughed on. "What does this ghost want? Why does it want the family to move away so badly? And what kind of ghost would be able to do these things?"

The guests were hanging on Zaiba's every word. All but one, who was starting to shuffle backwards out of the room. Zaiba pretended not to notice – this person needed to be caught in the act. Zaiba's glance flickered over towards Ali, stood at a discreet distance from the door, ready for his next cue.

"Well, the answer lies in the fact that this wasn't a ghost at all. And this is no ghost story. Because the true culprit of these crimes is ... Alexandra!"

Poppy flicked on the lights again and Zaiba pointed to Ali at the back of the room. He was standing at an angle with a large mirror in his hands. In the reflection, the guests clearly saw Alexandra, one hand still on the doorknob, trying to sneak out of the back door!

She would have got away too, if Aunt Fouzia hadn't been standing on the other side, ready to intercept her. Zaiba's heart lifted when she saw her auntie, wrapped in her furry purple dressing gown and hair in a loose long braid, yet still looking absolutely fearsome. It may have been her bedtime but Aunt Fouzia always managed to be in the right place at the right time!

"Oh no, you don't!" Aunt Fouzia grabbed Alexandra by the arm and marched her back into the room, planting her firmly in front of the police chief who was struggling to get to his feet.

Two other police officers followed her through the back door and Zaiba was surprised, but Aunt Fouzia winked at her. "I thought the chief might need some backup too."

The police officers each held one of Alexandra's arms as the chief put her in handcuffs. Her face was deathly pale and her gaze remained fixed on Zaiba. She looked furious, embarrassed, apologetic and defiant all at once.

"W—why would you do this?" Jack stammered at Alexandra. "I thought we were friends?"

Alexandra kept her mouth tightly shut, but under the pressure of every eye in the room staring at her, she broke down. "I have a lot of debts, OK!" she spat out. "My company needs the money! We just lost a huge deal. If we could buy this land and turn this old place into a block of flats, we'd make a killing."

Sefi and Max gasped at the horror of imagining Oakwood Manor torn down to the ground.

"How did you even manage to cause all this mayhem?" Jack seemed disgusted at the thought of Alexandra creeping around their house. Alexandra remained silent so Zaiba stepped forwards.

"You know the secret passageway in the library you told us about? It leads out into the grounds, by the pond. It looks like it's been boarded up but it's easy to move them aside to access the house. She even put her own padlock on the iron grille on the outside entrance. I bet you'll find the key on her."

The police chief patted Alexandra down and sure enough, in her trouser pocket, found a small silver key on a ring. He also pulled out a shiny bracelet that had been attached to the keyring.

"My bracelet!" Courtney gasped, delighted to be reunited with her jewellery.

Zaiba grinned, thrilled she'd been correct about the key but even happier that Courtney's bracelet had been returned.

"Alexandra has been using that tunnel to enter the manor to cause the 'hauntings', like moving the furniture around. We found one of her *original handmade* earrings inside the passage."

Alexandra's hand instinctively darted up to her ears.

She was wearing a pair of earrings, one of them similar to the one Zaiba had found.

"I can't believe you would damage our possessions and misuse our house like that." Courtney's voice wavered with emotion.

"Oh, why do you care?!" Alexandra hissed. "This place is falling apart anyway."

Courtney stepped forwards, holding on to Olivia and Flora's hands tightly.

"This is our home." She looked Alexandra dead in the eye and soon the criminal fell silent. "We will never leave it." Flora and Olivia looked up into their mother's face and hugged her. Jack came over and put an arm round Courtney's shoulder.

Alexandra was put in handcuffs and led away by the officer that had come with Aunt Fouzia. Zaiba noticed the police chief was awkwardly hanging around by the door, glancing over at her, so she sighed and walked over to him.

"Well, Zaiba, it seems you've helped us out here –" the chief went red – "again. Some of the other officers down at the station asked if you could uh, come in one day and tell them about your group."

"You mean the Snow Leopard Detective Agency UK branch," Zaiba smiled, politely correcting him.

"That's right. They said they're fans."

"I would love to!" Zaiba beamed and the police chief seemed relieved. He gave her an enthusiastic handshake and then went out to the police car to check on Alexandra.

Zaiba walked back into the room where the guests were discussing the events of the evening. No one could believe that the woman they'd been speaking to all evening was a criminal!

"She's given a bad name to those of us who work in property," Zaiba overheard Laurence bellow at Isabela and Anita who looked thoroughly fed up.

One police officer had stayed behind to take statements from everyone and she came up to Zaiba first. Her face seemed very familiar.

"I think we met before at the Royal Star Hotel," Zaiba said. "When I solved the case of the missing diamond dog collar?"

The officer's face suddenly lit up. "Of course! Zaiba! You are quite the detective, congratulations. Would you mind talking me through the events of the evening?"

Zaiba nodded eagerly. "I'd love to. But would you mind taking the statement of that couple over there first?" Zaiba pointed out Isabela and Anita. "I really think they'd like to get home."

The officer smiled and agreed, promising Zaiba she'd come back to chat to her later.

Aunt Fouzia snuck up on Zaiba and gave her a huge, squeezy hug. Once again, Zaiba found herself wondering where her tiny auntie got all that strength from.

"Zaiba, you have made me so proud." Aunt Fouzia beamed down at her. "The Snow Leopard Detective Agency UK is in good hands."

"I couldn't have done it without my team," Zaiba replied and she beckoned over all her friends that had helped her that evening. Poppy, Ali, Olivia, Flora, Layla and Ade gathered round Zaiba, looking pleased as punch. They looked up at Aunt Fouzia, who wasn't much taller than them, with a mix of admiration and wonder. After her impressive appearance catching Alexandra at the door, she must have seemed like a superhero to Zaiba's friends who'd never met her before! This made Zaiba extremely proud.

"My, my, my." Aunt Fouzia took in all their faces. "Your team keeps getting bigger every time I see you!"

Zaiba chuckled. "I know. But it might be a problem."

Poppy and Ali suddenly looked worried. "Why?"

"Well, it's our HQ." Zaiba smiled. "I'm going to need to get a bigger desk."

16
A SLEEPOVER
TO REMEMBER

"Agent's log, it's 22:30 hours." Zaiba yawned. "The
culprit, Alexandra, has been apprehended by police.
The evidence has been handed over and the case is
closed."

"Zaiba, are you coming to say goodbye to everyone?"
Poppy shouted from the foyer.

Zaiba yawned again and switched off her voice
recorder, sitting up wearily from the sofa. Now that
the police were gone, the guests were free to leave
and finally get some sleep. Zaiba walked out into the
foyer where Poppy was chatting with Olivia and Ade.
Ali and Flora had finally managed to get hold of the

encyclopedia to look up 'circumstantial evidence' and were discussing their findings on the stairs. Zaiba giggled at her little brother, but she was very pleased he'd found a friend who shared his love for knowledge.

Thankfully Isabela and Anita had managed to leave after the police spoke to them, but not before they managed to invite Courtney and Jack over for tea next weekend. Layla was fast asleep by the time Jay was able to leave and he had carried her out to the car, promising Jack to come over next week to help him put up a fence. Zaiba was thrilled that Courtney and Jack had found some new friends in their neighbours – ones who would make them feel right at home here.

At the door, Sefi and Max had grabbed hold of Ade and were making moves to leave. "Once again, I really want to apologize for how we were at the beginning of the evening." Sefi took Courtney's hand in hers. "We're so pleased you are the new owners of Oakwood Manor."

Max put a hand on Ade's shoulder. "And you kids must be a lot of fun. I've never seen Ade off his phone for so long before."

"Dad!" Ade groaned, looking highly embarrassed. But once they were outside, Ade sent a message through to the group chat.

Cool evening. Count me in for any future investigations!

He'd caught the detective bug all right.

Zaiba scooted up next to Aunt Fouzia, who was chatting with Hassan and Jessica as they put on their coats.

"Auntie, is Sam OK? I hope you having to come here at night hasn't stressed her." Zaiba had heard that stress could be bad for an expectant mother.

"Oh, she's fine, you little star." Aunt Fouzia stroked Zaiba's head. "In fact, I was just telling your mum and dad that she's decided on a name!"

Zaiba could barely contain her excitement. "What is it? What is it?"

Poppy and Ali had overheard and they came running up too, looking up at Aunt Fouzia with huge smiles.

"The baby will be called Nabiha."

Poppy clapped her hands together. "So pretty!"

But Zaiba was stunned. "But that was my—"

"Ammi's name." Hassan smiled. "Samirah wanted to name the baby after her auntie."

Zaiba beamed so hard she felt like she'd never stop.

"Do you like it?" Aunt Fouzia smiled.

Zaiba nodded and squeezed her dad hard. "I love it. And I'm sure Ammi would love it too."

Once all the other guests had left, it was sleepover time. Jack and Courtney were thoroughly exhausted and gave the children strict instructions not to wake them up before 9a.m. in the morning.

Cramming into Olivia's bathroom, the five kids brushed their teeth (for exactly two minutes as Ali and Flora insisted this was the dentist's recommended time) and took it in turns to spit into the sink. Though Ali narrowly missed Zaiba's face.

"You did that on purpose!" Zaiba gasped and flicked Ali with the corner of a towel.

"I didn't, I promise!" her brother objected, but he

couldn't help but break into giggles.

Once they were all clean they raced into the bedroom and into their sleeping bags.

"OK," Olivia announced. "You have to put your PJs on inside the covers, whoever gets them on first wins!"

"Wins what?" Flora asked.

"Nothing, you just *win*," Olivia replied. "Three, two, one, go!"

There was a lot of squirming and wiggling, and Zaiba found it particularly difficult to get her socks off without climbing all the way down inside her sleeping bag. After about thirty seconds of pulling and shoving she heard...

"Ta-da!"

Poppy had leaped out of her sleeping bag and was posing in the middle of the room. She had changed into her all-in-one PJ's decorated like the night sky in record time.

There was a soft knock at the door and Courtney appeared. "OK, everyone. Time for bed now. Sleep tight and remember, no waking up before nine." She blew them a kiss and turned out the light. Zaiba wasn't too worried about waking up early, she was exhausted.

"Can we keep the nightlight on?" Olivia asked drowsily, tucked up inside her sleeping bag.

"Why? Are you afraid there might be *ghostssss*?" Flora teased.

"No! I just don't like the dark." Olivia yawned.

"Neither do I," came Ali's voice well within the folds of his huge sleeping bag.

Poppy flicked on the glowing moon that was plugged into the wall and snuggled down inside her sleeping bag.

"I'm just ready to get my beauty rest," she sighed. "Today was epic."

"It was," Zaiba agreed. "There's just one last thing on my mind... How did those dressmaker's dummies fall on Flora?"

There was a moment of silence before Flora poked her head above her covers. "Um, actually, what happened was ... I just tripped and fell into them. I was too embarrassed to say at the time, and then that scream rang out before I had chance."

Despite their sleepiness, the whole gang burst into laughter at Flora's clumsiness.

"I suppose that solves *that* mystery," Zaiba chuckled, closing her eyes. "Goodnight, team."

"*Niiight*," Poppy sang.

"Goodnight." Olivia was already falling asleep.

"Uh, Zaiba what's that?" Zaiba opened her eyes and Ali was pointing at the wall behind her.

Olivia, Zaiba and Poppy all sat up straight in bed to see...

Two ghostly shadowy figures floating on the wall!

"AARGH!" the three girls screamed, throwing their covers over their heads.

Flora and Ali burst into fits of giggles!

Zaiba glanced over at the shadowy figures once again and realized that Flora was using the nightlight to make shadow puppets on the walls with her hands!

"You cheeky little weasels!" Poppy threw a cushion at Ali.

"There's only one way to settle this." Zaiba narrowed her eyes. "PILLOW FIGHT!"

By the time the fight was over and the winners confirmed (Zaiba, Poppy and Olivia), it had gone past midnight.

They scrambled back into their sleeping bags and one by one their eyes closed.

As the sound of Ali's little snores drifted across the room, Zaiba counted the sleeping detectives – there were so many of them! The Snow Leopard Detective Agency-UK would soon need sub-divisions. Maybe she could promote Poppy and Ali? Phew! Running a detective agency was hard work, but she wouldn't change it for the world.

As Zaiba's eyes grew heavy and finally closed, she wondered what their next mystery would be to solve. Maybe baby Nabiha would be born by then. *A baby detective*, was Zaiba's last thought before she fell asleep. *Now wouldn't that be something?*

DO YOU HAVE WHAT IT TAKES
TO JOIN ZAIBA AND THE SNOW
LEOPARD DETECTIVE AGENCY?

TURN THE PAGE
TO FIND OUT!

AGENT ZAIBA'S TOP DETECTIVE TIPS

🔍 Be prepared! Have everything you might need with you. You never know when you might need to bag up evidence or take finger prints...

🔍 Careful observation – it's important to take note of everything (and everyone) you notice, and something things that aren't there but should be.

🔍 Organisation – Ali might roll his eyes at Zaiba's investigation boards but it's useful to have all the information in one and place and to see how everything connects together! You could use sticky notes, or a pin board with string.

🔍 Delegation and trust – fortunately Zaiba has a team she can depend on! Give team members tasks based on their skills. It's important to have eyes and ears everywhere, so you don't miss a thing

🔍 Responsibility – you are responsible for your fellow detectives so don't ask them to do anything that you wouldn't do, and make sure everyone is confident in their tasks!

THE HISTORY OF OAKWOOD MANOR

The Booker family are fascinated by the history of Oakwood Manor – from its role in World War One to a site for women's football teams to train. Here's some more history!

WAR HOSPITALS

After the outbreak of World War One, despite preparations, England wasn't ready for the number of wounded men brought back from battle. The War Office had predicted that they'd need 50,000 beds, when in fact 73,000 soldiers needed to be in hospital. To help with the lack of beds, some owners of country houses offered them as convalescent homes for the soldiers to recover after being treated.

A real-life example of this is Blenheim Palace in Oxfordshire. The family donated their home as a war hospital in 1914. The Long Library became a ward, with fifty beds for injured soldiers. A surgery room was also created, and a reading room – just for the soldiers.

WOMEN'S FOOTBALL

The first women's football match was in 1895 and the game really flourished in the 1920s with around 150 women's teams in England.

One of the first female professionals was Lily Parr. She was a winger and played for the Dick Kerr's Ladies team, named after the munitions factory in Preston where most of the team worked during the first World War. They were the first women's team to play wearing shorts and the first to go on a tour overseas. On Boxing Day 1920, a crowd of 53,000 came to watch them play, and there were thousands of fans outside. That is more than most men's games now.

However, in December 1921, women's football was effectively banned by the Football Association, who wouldn't let the women play on FA-affiliated pitches, claiming that "the game of football is quite unsuitable for females and ought not to be encouraged".

It wasn't until 1971 that the ban was lifted, following the formation of the Women's Football Association (WFA) in 1969. For half a century women's football was held back. Now it's going from strength to strength, with a friendly match between England Women and Germany Women selling out the 90,000 capacity Wembley Stadium in 2019.

WHAT ARE JINN?
AND ARE THEY REAL...

In Islamic mythology, jinn are supernatural creatures like spirits, ghosts or demons. They can appear as many things like animals, winds, shadows or humans. The idea of jinn originated in the Middle East in ancient times, and nowadays many people who live in Islamic countries believe in jinn. In the Quran, which is the holy book of Muslims, it says that God created the jinn before humans from 'smokeless fire'.

Jinn live in an invisible world parallel to ours and behave similarly to humans. Like us they are said to eat and drink, marry, have children and die. Jinn can be good or bad, and this is shown by how they choose to use their powers. Jinn can take on the form of anything they want to, for example a snake, a tree or a human. They might use this ability to trick people or scare people, like the suspected ghost in Oakwood Manor.

As with all supernatural beings, whether you believe in jinn or not is a matter of opinion. Some people, like Ali and Olivia, don't believe in jinn, as there isn't a way to scientifically prove they exist. But others, like Zaiba, keep an open mind as there are many unknown things in our world.

SUPER SLEEPOVERS!

Zaiba, Poppy and Olivia love sleepovers!
Here are some of their favourite things to do...

🔍 PILLOW FIGHT! Make sure you have enough space (and there's nothing breakable nearby). It's a good idea to have a few rules, like avoiding faces. Then go for it!

🔍 Play Murder in the Dark – the perfect game to test your detective skills! You need playing cards – enough for one per player. One card should be an ace and one a face card, the rest numbers. Whoever gets the ace is the detective and can reveal their card. The face card is the killer and takes out other players by winking at them. The detective has to identify the killer before it's too late!

🔍 Shadow puppets – you can make your own shadow puppets out of cardboard or use your hands to create shapes! You'll need a lamp and a bare wall. Point the lamp at the wall and place your puppets in between them and make the shadows come to life!

STUFFED ALOO BURGERS

Make stuffed aloo burgers so good that your party guests will never want to leave!

Learn how to make Hassan's delicious stuffed aloo burgers! Just make sure that you wash your hands properly before you begin, like Ali insists. This recipe uses knives and the oven, so ask an adult to help.

Ingredients

- 4 medium potatoes
- 60g chopped cashews
- 60g desiccated coconut
- 1tsp turmeric
- 1tsp chilli powder
- 1tsp cumin powder
- 1tsp salt
- 1tsp pepper
- 150g fine breadcrumbs
- Fresh coriander to garnish

Method

1. Wash and peel the potatoes. Cut the potatoes into chunks.

2. Boil the potaties for around 15 minutes, or until soft.

3. Combine potatoes and all spices in a bowl. Mash together.

4. Scoop out some of the potato mixture and mould into a flat circle. Take a spoonful of the cashews and coconut, and place in the middle. Take another scoop of potato and cover the filling, forming one whole round patty. If you are cooking them in the oven, they should be roughly 1 inch thick. If you are frying them they should be around 2cm thick.

5. Pour the breadcrumbs on to a plate.

6. Take the patties and cover all sides in the breadcrumbs.

7. To cook the patties in the oven, place on a lightly-oiled baking-sheet and cook for 20 minutes at 180 degrees. Flip them over halfway so both sides turn golden brown.

8. To cook on the hob, fry the patties in oil until they are golden brown on both sides.

9. Chop up the fresh coriander and sprinkle over the top.

10. Choose whatever accompaniments you'd like! You could put these in burger buns or naan with salad and chutneys. Or with chips and salad on the side. This bit is up to you!

11. Eat and enjoy!

HASSAN AND ALI'S HILARIOUS JOKES

Who solves penguin crimes?

The pol-ice!

Which part of a tree does a dog like best?

The bark!

What do you call a group of dead naughty rodents?

Polter-mice!

How do you know when a sea bird is tired?

it's puffin!

Why did the underwear go to jail?

They were knickers!

Why was the piece of cheddar booed off stage?

His jokes were too cheesy!

SEE HOW THE SNOW LEOPARD
DETECTIVE AGENCY (UK BRANCH!)
SOLVED THEIR FIRST MYSTERY IN...

Agent Zaiba
INVESTIGATES

THE MISSING DIAMONDS

I
MEHNDI MADNESS

"Detective's log number thirty five. The time is..." Zaiba glanced at her watch. "15:00 hours. Location: The Royal Star Hotel, Farnworth, the United Kingdom. Observation and hiding point secured. This is Agent Zaiba."

Zaiba shuffled further back beneath an empty dining table, clutching her favourite book of all time, *Eden Lockett's Detective Handbook*. Eden Lockett might be made up, but her books were based on real crimes and she could teach a budding detective anything they needed to know about sleuthing. In her mysteries, she'd battled robbers and escaped tigers, a ghost in a mansion and villains in a circus. Zaiba flicked through the pages.

There! Advice about blending in with your surroundings: *Avoid bright colours. Now is not the time to make a fashion statement.*

Zaiba glanced down at her outfit. She was wearing a shiny blue shalwar kameez with a silver dupatta tossed over one shoulder. Hmmm. The perfect outfit for a pre-wedding Mehndi party sure, but when trying to hide from her arch nemesis? Not so good.

Although perhaps arch nemesis was a *bit* too harsh. Zaiba's cousin, Mariam, was on the other side of the room sandwiched between her parents. At least she had been on Zaiba's last sweep of the room. Things had been tense between them ever since Mariam decided to be born on the exact same day as Zaiba. Well, one year later. But couldn't she have waited a day or two at least? The latest incident in the growing feud had been at their annual joint birthday party last week. Mariam had accused Zaiba of hitting the unicorn piñata too hard. Seriously – how could anyone hit a piñata *too* hard? Zaiba could practically feel Mariam's icy stare piercing through the tablecloth, sending a shiver down her spine.

She turned the page in *Eden Lockett's Detective Handbook* to read one of many notes scribbled in the margin. She traced a finger round the familiar loops and curls. This and the mystery stories had been her mum's and she'd made lots of comments across her beloved book collection. Now they belonged to Zaiba, who had spent hours searching for each unique scribbling. It was her special way of getting to know her mum, who she called Ammi.

This message was a particular favourite of hers:

Better put on my brave pants today!

Zaiba smiled to herself. Her ammi had been funny. At least, she *thought* she had been funny. She'd passed away when Zaiba was too young to remember. Whenever Zaiba tried to ask her dad about what happened, he would repeat the same phrase, "Leave the past in the past." She always had the feeling that there was something her dad wasn't telling her. Something left to uncover...

Zaiba refocused her mind and peered out from beneath the tablecloth. Beyond the dining table the party was getting busier. Even though the event had officially started quite a while ago, three o'clock was still considered early for a party that would go on into the early hours of the morning. The guests that had just arrived, wearing jewel-coloured saris and sharply tailored suits, chatted in groups, catching up on all the latest news. The women's bangles cascaded down their wrists as they danced with their partners beside the patio doors that opened on to the garden. But there was no sign of Mariam, thank goodness.

Mariam had better not ruin this party too, Zaiba thought. Zaiba knew that Samirah, another of her cousins, had spent months planning her Mehndi party. She'd wanted it to be the perfect party in the run-up to the perfect wedding, where Samirah – or Sam, as most people called her – would be the perfect bride. Sam liked perfect.

Zaiba relaxed a little and gave a sigh of pleasure – it was all so pretty! A Pakistani wedding was nothing without a Mehndi party beforehand, where the bride has parts of her body decorated in elaborate patterns with a red dye called henna. There would be choreographed dancing, special sweets fed to the bride and, importantly, her female relatives would share their advice for a happy marriage.

This party definitely had the three main ingredients for a successful Mehndi party in abundance – food, music and dancing! At the top of the room on a little stage was Sam. As the bride-to-be, she sat on a gilded white lounge chair, wearing a sari in deep red, orange and yellow. Zaiba saw her cousin stifle a yawn as she continued to sit patiently while her hands were decorated with the henna. Meanwhile her fiancé, Tanvir, had been cornered next to the punchbowl by some eager aunties who wanted to know *everything* about the upcoming wedding. It seemed at the moment that this party was fun for everyone *but* the young couple.

Zaiba felt a stab of sadness. Sam was her favourite cousin and Zaiba wanted this evening to be everything she'd hoped it would be. She glanced around the room, taking a mental note of as many details as possible. As the linen curtains swelled in the breeze, she noticed that the patio doors opened *out* on to the garden, rather than *in* to the room. That could be useful information if they were involved in a high-stakes chase! There was a main entrance leading out on to the drive too. She eased a little gold pencil that the receptionist had given her out of her bag and added extra details to the hotel map she'd drawn that morning. The receptionist — "Liza with a 'z'!" — had taken Zaiba and some of the other children round the hotel while their parents were busy unpacking. She'd pointed out the twenty-six bedrooms, the library with its leather-bound books and the extensive hotel grounds and separate buildings.

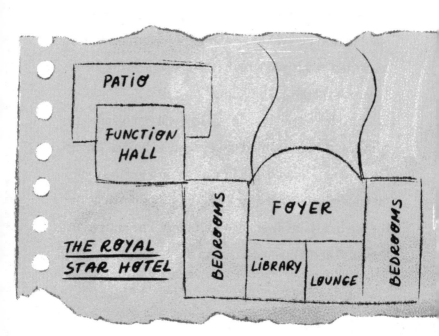

Zaiba opened the phone's voice recorder again and put it to her lips. "Observations: number of guests one, two, three, four, five ... uhhhh, at least fifty people. Sofas and soft seating at ninety degrees to my right. Most people are on the dance floor. Bad – no *really* bad – music from the DJ booth close to the north-east window. No suspicious activity so far—"

"Apart from the girl hiding under the dining table!"

The tablecloth whipped up and a hand reached for Zaiba, pulling her swiftly out from her observation point.

"Aunt Fouzia!" Zaiba groaned, annoyed that she'd been discovered. Sam's mum was a tiny lady who somehow possessed the strength of a bodybuilder. Zaiba liked to imagine this strength came from all the extra-strong cups of chai Aunt Fouzia got through in a day – her record was ten! Zaiba quickly stashed away her phone, pencil and *Eden Lockett's Detective Handbook* in a little yellow purse she wore across her body. The hotel map was tucked carefully between the back pages of her book. A detective never knew when they might need a map!

"What are you doing sneaking about under there?" her aunt chided gently. "It's time for your family dance. And by the look on Samirah's face, she needs the entertainment. That henna artist is taking far too long!" Sam was Aunt Fouzia's eldest daughter and she was a doctor – "the youngest on her ward!" as Aunt Fouzia liked to remind people.

Zaiba had always looked up to Sam. She was clever and sophisticated and Zaiba often thought she could have been a spy if she'd wanted to be, like in the movies. She looked especially impressive today, if a little bit bored. As Zaiba glanced over at Samirah and Tanvir (or SamTan as Zaiba had decided their couple name was), she noticed the golden tikka hanging over Sam's forehead. It sparkled with rubies and sapphires, making Sam look like royalty.

"If I ever wear one of those, make sure I remember to hire a personal security team," Zaiba noted.

"Today the security is us," Aunt Fouzia teased. "Now come on, let's kick off this song and dance competition! Wait – where's Poppy?"

Poppy had been Zaiba's best friend for longer than she could remember. Since she was practically family she had been invited along to the party too. That morning Poppy's parents had dropped her off just in time for the tour of the hotel. Zaiba had lent Poppy one of her green silk dupattas to wear with her favourite party dress and Poppy had insisted on the matching green khussa. Parties involved two of Poppy's favourite things – dressing up and free food. Throw in a glamorous hotel and she was in heaven. This hotel in particular was right up her street. Liza had told them on their tour that it was built by some fancy-pants Lord ages ago. Zaiba thought he must have been a show-off since he had his home built like a mini castle, complete with three turrets that towered into the sky.

"Poppy! Over here!" Zaiba called, spotting her best friend over by a plate of brightly coloured burfi.

Poppy shoved the last sweet crumbs into her mouth and ran up to join Zaiba and a small group of children next to the dance floor.

Poppy linked her arm through Zaiba's as they

waited for three grannies to finish their routine to a famous Bollywood love song. "Did you complete your observations?" she asked Zaiba. "I was doing mine ... over by the chocolate fountain..."

Zaiba laughed. "I *was* doing them before Aunt Fouzia found me." She turned to her aunt. "How *did* you find me, by the way?"

"A great agent never reveals their secrets." Aunt Fouzia tapped the side of her nose. Zaiba's aunt was even more famous than Eden Lockett, in Karachi at least. She ran the **Snow Leopard Detective Agency** – the best agency in Pakistan. She'd encouraged Zaiba to read her first Eden Lockett mystery after Zaiba had asked one too many questions about Aunt Fouzia's job. Now Zaiba *and* Poppy were mega fans. Zaiba had Eden Lockett bed covers, Eden Lockett stationery... Aunt Fouzia had even found her an Eden Lockett phone case! Zaiba would call her aunt in Pakistan and they would talk for hours about their hero's latest adventure. Sometimes Zaiba thought that Aunt Fouzia loved the books even more than she did.

"She saw you because your feet were poking out!" Zaiba's younger half-brother Ali chimed in, wriggling between Zaiba and Poppy. "How long will we all have to dance until Sam's Mehndi is finished?"

"I heard you're top of your class in maths, Ali. How long do *you* think it will take?" Aunt Fouzia tested him.

Ali tapped a finger against his chin as he counted. "Hmmm, each hand would take around twenty minutes, then double that for the feet, plus drying time..."

"So, have you had any thrilling cases to solve recently, Auntie?" Zaiba asked, squeezing her aunt's hand while her brother's eyes darted around the room, making rapid calculations.

"You know I can't discuss any of my cases." Aunt Fouzia pursed her lips. "But let's just say, the prime minister owes me a big favour..."

"*The prime minister!*" the girls gasped. Aunt Fouzia was definitely the real deal. What could the crisis have been this time? Ten Bengal tigers let loose in parliament?

"... then the song and dance contest would have

to go on for one hour and fifty minutes!" said Ali triumphantly.

"Brilliant, Ali." Aunt Fouzia patted his cheek. "You'd better get dancing!"

The music for the grannies' dance finished and the whole room erupted into applause.

"Zaiba, Ali, there you are," came a warm voice from behind them. It was Zaiba's stepmum Jessica, who she called Mum, and she was ready to dance. "It's the moment we've been practising for!"

"I think I'll just watch this one, Mum." Zaiba wasn't much of a dancer, and besides, she couldn't keep up her safety observations and dance at the same time.

"What?" her mum cried. "But we've been working on it all week!" Zaiba's mum hadn't realized that the song and dance contest was supposed to be just a bit of fun. In fact she'd been taking it quite seriously, making the whole family stay up until late memorizing the choreography.

"I'll still perform, Mrs—Oh!" Poppy quickly shut up after Zaiba squeezed her hand.

But there wasn't time for Jessica to try and persuade them as the music had started and Zaiba's dad, Hassan, whisked Ali and Jessica on to the dance floor.

"Let's see those feet dancing," he grinned, shaking his hips to the beat.

JOIN ZAIBA ON HER ADVENTURES...

ABOUT THE AUTHOR

Annabelle Sami is a writer and performer.
She grew up next to the sea on the south coast of the
UK and moved to London, where she now lives, for
university. At Queen Mary University she had an amazing
time studying English Literature and Drama, finally
graduating with an MA in English Literature.

When she isn't writing she enjoys playing saxophone
in a band with her friends, performing live art
and swimming in the sea!

ABOUT THE ILLUSTRATOR

Originally from Romania, Daniela Sosa now lives and works in Cambridge with her husband and is completing an MA in children's book illustration at the Cambridge School of Art.

Creating a magical mix of the ordinary and the unusual, Daniela enjoys highlighting subtle detail and finding beauty in everyday life. She gets inspiration from nature, books and observing the world around.

HELP ZAIBA SOLVE HER
NEXT CRIME IN...

Agent Zaiba
INVESTIGATES

THE SMUGGLER'S SECRET